GELSY

Danni Bayles-Yeager

illustrations by Tom Kinnee

ISBN: 978-1-4907-4522-0 (sc)
ISBN: 978-1-4907-4523-7 (e)

Library of Congress Control Number: 2014915179

Trafford rev. 09/04/2014

 www.trafford.com

North America & international
toll-free: 1 888 232 4444 (USA & Canada)
fax: 812 355 4082

Dedicated to
Leonard Nimoy
for
Kid Monk Baroni

-1-

"Mister, that's the last bus over there!" A freshman in a hoodie tried to get the attention of the strange older dude, in his late twenties, reading notices on the kiosk.

David glanced up with a "Huh" and then, "Thanks, I just got here" and went back to reading.

"OK man, but you gotta be careful with this bus system on week-ends. They shut down early." With that sage piece of advice the hooded one hopped on the last bus out of UCSM and was gone.

David looked back up to find himself alone on the landing. It would be getting dark soon. No sense putting it off any longer. He was really and truly here. He'd better find the dorm.

There wasn't much luggage, but what he had was awkward, mostly books and old class binders he couldn't make himself throw away. Clothes and other personal items made up so little he could have balanced that bag on his head. The rest he had to drag in an old steamer trunk up from the bus stop to where the path joined with the main walkway, then onto the arched bridge over a stream that cut across the campus.

There he stopped for a moment. The sun was just starting to set. From where he was standing he knew from the guidebooks he could look slightly downhill, right into the windows of his lab. Yes, that's where he would be working for the next two years with the biochemist Dr. Robert Chaveral. *The* Dr. Robert Chaveral.

Turning around, he knew the window he was looking directly into had to be to the main Dance Room. Not that he was all that interested in dance, but it gave him a satisfaction to be so new to campus and yet be able to tell where

1

everything was. The dance building was the last building he had to pass before reaching his dorm. As he stared into the big empty room, he realized it wasn't empty anymore. A lone figure had taken a position at the far end of the barre and was warming up, looking into a small sliver of mirror across the room.

The sun shifted in its final descent and threw a beam into it, causing the light to ricochet off the mirror backing the barre and throwing a projected image of the dancer on the wall facing David. She had just begun to bend forward. Now the light came up her back leg, rose to the ceiling to form a vertical line with her supporting leg as her hand gracefully brushed the floor, then lifted. For less than a second the image was there on the wall with the girl's chin and hand parallel to the floor, as if she'd fly away, her leg still stretched to the heavens. Then the sun sank and the image was gone.

But David felt as though it was a personal omen. His time here would be the high point of his life. He was certain of the image's significance – it meant his career would grow and fly.

Picking up his bags and steamer trunk he continued the short distance to Melville Hall.

Not until months later would he realize only one dancer on campus could take an *arabesque panché* like that.

-2-

Melville Hall was brand-new yet looked exactly like what it was. It could have been built in the 1960s or '80s, practically any period at all. *A dorm is a dorm is a dorm*, David thought as he dragged his bags across the threshold of this one.

Inside the lobby area was a desk marked Student Assistant. Behind the desk, reading, was a short, stout, Hispanic youth whose partially-shaved head was already showing signs of male-pattern baldness. He looked up at David with a mild mixture of amusement and irritation.

"Please tell me you're a TA or at least somebody higher up the food chain than me so I don't have to get ballistic at you for checking in late. You're obviously older than I am. Come on. Ex-military, am I right?"

David shook the young man's hand; gave him one of his rare, almost-bitter smiles, then threw himself into a chair. "Very good. Right on both counts. I'm David Collins, ex-army and a brand-new TA. I'm sorry about the 'late' part; just had to do a little sightseeing on my way here."

"Forgiven this time. My name is Gordie Gomez. Who do you TA for?"

"Dr. Robert Chaveral."

David said this with a little tinge of pride but really had no idea if the young man knew who Dr. Chaveral was. Then he noticed the manual on chemical reactions shaking in the young man's hands. Gordie stood up suddenly and called into the lobby, "*Mark*, damn it... come over here, like, NOW!"

A tall man about Gordie's age, even skinnier than David, unfolded himself from a padded chair which had held uncountable student bodies and shuffled over their way.

"Do you know who this is?" Gordie asked pointedly of him.

The watery eyes scanned David with casual intensity. "No, can't say I do. But he's new and must be quite special for you to take such an interest, Gordie."

"Damned straight. *This*, my friend, is David Collins, Chaveral's new TA." Gordie fell back into his chair. "Do we kill him now, or later… on the roof, where no one can see?"

"No, Gordie, we talk to the stranger." Mark considered this briefly before pulling up a chair.

"Get him to tell us his secrets. Learn from him."

"Whoa, guys! What are we talking about here? Remember, I'm the new guy in town."

David was beginning to feel like everyone was speaking a foreign language.

The other two just stared at him, then Gordie yielded the stage to Mark. "First question I guess we both have is, what kind of 'hook' did you use on your application?" Mark asked.

Now David was positive about the foreign language part. This made no sense.

"What, my college application?"

"No, dummy, your application to Chaveral. For the *job*. The TA position.

What 'hook' did you use?"

David stared at him blankly.

Gordie spoke up helpfully, "Maybe it would help, Mark, if he knew that both of us, plus about two hundred other extremely gifted future scientists from around the world, were fighting over that choice position and each one of us was trying to come up with some kind of angle to make our applications stand out from the rest. We just want to know, how did you *do it*?!"

David looked dazed, "Applications?"

Mark grabbed Gordie's arm to stop him from saying anything else and gave David a long look. "Yes,

5

David, applications. You did *apply* for the position of TA, didn't you?"

"Well, no, not really--"

"What the…" was all Gordie could get out before Mark's hand was clamped firmly across his mouth. "Please go on, David," he smiled gently.

"When I got out of the army, I had some community college credits, practically enough to get an AA, so a counselor suggested I take the tests and go directly into Carmichael State. I'd been really interested in biochemistry, got good grades, and I was lucky enough to get Dr. Latchke as my instructor. My master's project was selected to be shown at your New Scientists Fair last spring, and Latchke is a good friend of Robert's. They took me out to dinner after I gave my presentation and the next thing I knew Robert casually mentioned his old TA was leaving and he was looking for someone to replace him. Would I be interested? Would I?!" David felt a little nervous at the rapt attention from the other two. "A doctoral program went along with the deal, so of course I was interested. I had no – repeat, *NO* – idea there was a bidding war up for the job!"

"Oh… my… Lord…in…heaven" Gordie cranked out one syllable at a time, while holding his head in his hands. Mark simply sat in his chair and gazed off into the ether.

"I was right, Gordo, *mi amigo*. There is much to be learned from this stranger."

-3-

David was barely settled into his room when Gordie appeared at his door announcing that his shift as "hall monitor" was over and he'd take the new TA over to the biochem lab. They walked past Mark, who had taken over Gordie's seat, with a nod and continued out the door and toward the bridge. There David hesitated.

He felt it was like a lucky charm; look into the dance room and get a clue of what the day would be like. Now the floor was concentrated on a tight group of male dancers in boots and Spanish-style sashes. The two men on the bridge could barely make out the figures of girls grouped in the back of the room.

"It's flamenco class," Gordie said. "My sister, Luisa, is somewhere in the back. See the guy in front?" he pointed to an exceptionally good-looking, lean Hispanic youth. "That's Rennie, Renaldo Montez. Luisa is so in love with him. He lived with my family for a few months after his mom died so he could graduate from high school with his class, but we were never buddies. Luisa will do his homework for him, darn the holes in his tights. Anything, man! Wasted! He's in love with his lead dancer, who can barely tolerate him." Gordie stifled a laugh.

They watched the dancers for a few minutes. The sound of Spanish guitar music floated faintly through an open window, along with the rhythmic *thunk-clack, clack* of the men's boots as they made their tight, stomping turns. Following their handsome leader, they managed to look like real gypsies. *Rennie may be a jerk*, David thought, *but he's one hell of a dancer.*

They walked on to the lab and David got the courage to ask, "Why are you being so nice to me, Gordie, if I got the job you wanted?"

Gordie smiled. "How did I know you were going to ask that? OK, because I knew it was a long shot? Not true. I was the leading candidate. In fact, I thought I had the job in my pocket. You were a real kick in the ass, David."

They reached an immense outdoor display kiosk marked "Chemistry" with maps of the different programs and David came to a full halt. It was dark by now and the only lights came from the top of the sign. David took his time and studied the young man. Gordie took it all without wavering. "So what are you saying, Gordie? You really *do* want to throw me off the roof?"

"Mark and I talked it over. We both know Chaveral, whom you seem to call Robert, like he's an old drinking buddy, and we've never known him to make a wrong move. If he does something that seems erratic and you chalk it up to him just being an old hippie at heart, sooner or later you're going to find out what the real reason was and you're going to feel like an idiot." Gordie looked down at the ground.

"Remember that, David. This man is probably the smartest man we'll ever know in our lives. Maybe you think you already know it, but you don't. You couldn't have seen him in action as often as Mark and I have over the years, since we were undergrads! He hand-picked both of us, that's why we thought we had the lock on your job. If he gave it to you, then you've got something we don't. Something he needs. For some reason, he needs you here. This last big project of his is the most important thing in his life right now, and you figure in somehow."

David looked up at the hallway maps and thought about the thesis work he'd presented, how excited the respected Dr. Chaveral had been. How they'd walked down those halls and peeked into some of the labs while Robert began giving him a brief outline of the work he'd be doing there. It made sense.

David had felt he was onto something with his research, but wasn't sure what exactly. Now he realized that Robert knew, exactly.

Gordie could tell a connection had been made but didn't push for more information, just turned and continued walking into the building. "What the booby prize is, is that I get to be *your* assistant. Yes, I know that's unheard of, a TA having his own administrative assistant (you can just call me 'AdMan') but since this project is going to be so time-consuming and you're new to the campus, Chaveral wanted a third person as back-up. Actually, fourth. Mark will be *my* back-up too. Chaveral is such a softie, he couldn't leave us both out. We'll probably do a lot of the menial stuff like grading papers and cleaning up after the beginning students. Don't worry, we get paid. As you may have gathered, neither of us is wealthy so every little bit helps."

David gave one of his half-smiles. "Even the TA position itself doesn't exactly put you in the lap of luxury, Gordie – but I'm sure you knew that. Coming out of the army I'm used to scraping by. But if I eat and can get the books I need, I'll be OK."

"In that case, welcome to Humble Hall," Gordie grinned. "We can all be paupers with brilliant futures ahead of us together! With Chaveral as a mentor we're bound to be at least semi-successful in the academic world when we get out. Mark and I have already planned to team up in our research work. Who knows, maybe you'll join us."

"Wait until I get my feet on the ground. Now tell me more about the work we're doing here."

"You probably know more about the anti-aging compounds than I do. Chaveral's been working on different strains for years, and from his vast supply of energy – I'll tell you, David, he runs us young guys into the wall! – whatever elixir he's come up with must be working."

David looked deep in thought. "But my work was in reconstitution, not longevity… not in human life at all. I'm wondering where he's seeing a connection."

"Trust me, David, if he wanted you here this badly, then he saw a connection. Reconstitution? Wow, are you thinking what I'm thinking?"

"Can't be done, Gordie. Not my way, at least."

"Better let Chaveral make that call.

-4-

Gordie left David to look around a little more, after making sure he could find his way back to Melville on his own. It was nearly eight o'clock by the time David reached the bridge and he was amazed to find all the lights still on in the studio and what looked like a rehearsal. All the girls were barefoot, but dressed in matching pastel leotards and chiffon wrapped-skirts reaching to just below their knees. Their hair was pinned up, ballerina-style, and each wore a matching piece of fabric in her hair; one as a bandeau, one a bow, and the girl who was called out to lead them had an ashes-of-roses silk flower over her ear.

Standing there at the head of these beauties, she stood out as though a spotlight were trained on her head; a slim, tiny body that commanded everyone's attention by the very way it stood. Her face was tilted slightly to one side, arms hanging, relaxed, but gracefully ready to move. Then the music began.

David thought he'd never heard such a sweet, simple sound, just a violin progressing from one note to another, and yet each note called forth a movement from her body that blended in such sincerity you'd think her body was creating the music. She sank nearly to the ground into a curtsey and one leg drew a semi-circle on the floor until it was directly behind her. Then she lifted up on her supporting leg until she was nearly on the tips of her toes and her back leg was parallel to the floor... and stayed there longer than David believed possible.

He had to get closer. The music was so faint...and he could barely see the faces. Intently he searched out the area near the window with all the killing skills the army had given him.

A killer wasn't what he'd wanted to become. Being trained as a sniper after having Randy die in his arms was a soul-altering experience. The Special Forces took all his natural skills, his endurance, strength, his keen eye, and concentrated them on one object: shoot to kill. He'd learned to search out a locale, make his way to the spot without being noticed, take up a position, and wait. Just wait until another human being of the wrong ethnic origin, wearing the wrong kind of clothes, came into his sights.

An old oak was to the left of the window, with manzanita bushes lining the streambed... perfect. He dropped noiselessly over the left inland side of the bridge, happy he had no books or backpack with him. Hitting the ground was nothing. The ground was soft and it was only a drop of ten feet at best, nothing for an ex-soldier still in prime condition. Four long strides brought him to the oak and the momentum he built up took him up to a branch. He swung easily into a crook, which led to another branch which led to...

A sniper's nest. That's exactly what it was. *I've got to stop thinking like that*, but the nearness of the music made him feel calmer. He took a deep breath and leaned forward to watch.

The dancer had come down from her arabesque and performed another long slide to the side before slowly and calmly lifting that leg to ceiling as if it were something people did every day. Behind her the others followed as well as possible, but except for a little Hispanic girl David guessed was Gordie's sister, nobody came even close.

Best just to watch her, David reasoned as he settled back, making sure the foliage hid him completely while still giving him that one observation point he needed. *She's the best.*

The slim little dancer continued to build on the slow, swooping, almost geometric figures through each wrenching stroke of the violin until it slowed, hesitated, and finally drew out one last sad note. She sank to her knees, wrapped one arm around her waist and raised her other hand to point the way to heaven. David, entranced, leaned forward and sighed, *Girl.*

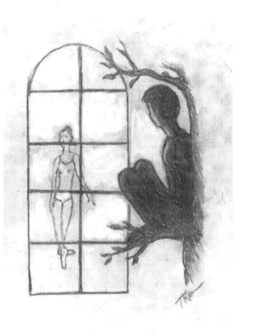

-5-

David never asked Gordie about the dancer, but as he got ready for classes to begin he learned a lot about the dance program as the two of them walked across the bridge to the lab.

The dancers had started early because every Christmastime they gave a benefit performance which raised most of their funding for the year, and starting with the other classes didn't give them enough time to rehearse. Yes, they were there at all hours because they had only the one main studio and two smaller rooms, mostly for dance-related classes. It was a tough program, and his sister struggled to make up all the academic credits she needed and still take all the required dance classes and rehearsals. All their toe shoes, which David was shocked were expensive and needed to be replaced often, had to be paid for by the dancers themselves. They bought all their own shoes, leotards and tights.

"Wow," David exhaled hard, "How does your sister afford all that? She obviously doesn't have time for a job!"

"So why do you think I wear so many hats, David? Hall monitor, adman, janitor… yes, I do that, too."

"Damn, Gordie! I've heard of brotherly love, but this takes the cake."

"Last Christmas Mark bought Luisa a pair of toe shoes, which is really funny because he's Jewish."

"Mark did that? Then there's hope even for his hard heart. I didn't realize he was Jewish."

"Well, he loves my little sister but she can't see him worth *caca* because of Rennie," Gordie groaned. "I don't think he'd convert, anyway. And I know *she* wouldn't. Why does religion have to be such a bummer sometimes?"

"You're talking to the wrong person. I ain't got *no* religion, and that's a fact. If I'd had any before, three tours of duty in Afghanistan would have cut it all out of me."

"Hell, I had no idea, David! What happened to you over there?"

They were sitting in Gordie's dorm room, having drunk several cold beers on a hot night or the conversation would never have gotten this far. David's eyes narrowed. "I don't like talking about it much. Let's just say I saw too many people die, then nearly got killed myself in an explosion. Spent nearly six months in a VA hospital so boring if it hadn't been for the correspondence college courses, I would have lost my mind. But I was luckier than most. I healed. Pretty soon I could start limping to regular classes on my own. After that, I knew I'd be OK…"

Here he looked down at his clenched fists. "Except for the post-traumatic stress syndrome disorder, Gordie. I should tell you that in case somebody calls you as hall monitor to report a guy's screaming like a banshee some night. I can still have problems, like battle nightmares…"

"Are you seeing somebody?"

"Yeah, the VA recommended me to a guy here on campus; a therapist who was in the Marines himself. Guess we'll have a lot to talk about." David gave a brief, apologetic laugh.

"Guess you will." Gordie was sympathetic but happily didn't continue.

First day of classes! "My first day to be a hot-shot TA," David looked at himself in the mirror after shaving and regarded his face more intently than he ever had. He was tall and lean, with broad shoulders knotted with muscle; some chest hair but only enough to look manly, not hirsute. It was his face he never much cared for.

It had an angular, ethnic look, but being orphaned left him without a clue to whether he was Native American, black Irish or what. Prominent cheekbones, rather thin lips that gave him a stern look, and dark brown eyes that could have been attractive if he didn't have the habit of constantly keeping them hooded like a hawk. He always thought he looked exactly like what the army had eventually made of him, a sniper. Killing men he'd never know anything about.

Before that he'd been a drill sergeant, and a good one. He'd been OK doing that job, but his marksmanship scores kept getting higher until the brass decided to put him in "shooting school." That was the beginning of the end. *Don't think about that now,* he told himself. *Robert told me to concentrate on my time as a sergeant, and to treat the new students like recruits. That I can do.* He quickly got dressed and headed out the door.

As usual, he stopped at the bridge. He'd deliberately left all his binders at the lab so he wouldn't be carrying anything and could drop over the edge and make his way to the nest. This was one of his favorite classes, the advanced ballet. David had soon learned that Rennie's "lead dancer" was "the Girl," and it sat right with him to remember Gordie saying Rennie was *barely tolerated* by his would-be lover. But in this class they would often dance together and David had to admit that it was magical. Rennie partnered the girl like she was made of porcelain and gold, or like she was a fairy princess or an angel from above. The girl responded with a gentle touch of assurance and a smile. Together they were beyond amazing.

This morning the girl was dressed in a lightly tie-dyed leotard of pinks and lavenders, with a tiny mauve chiffon skirt wrapped around her waist. Rennie was in his usual rag-bag assortment of leg-warmers, tights and a torn tee-shirt, but he could pull it off. They were working on allegro today... fast, flying steps to cheerful music. The girl could take to the air like a hummingbird. David liked hummingbirds so he took that as a good omen for his day in the classrooms and lab.

The music was a waltz; even David could tell that much. As little as he knew about most music, there was no mistaking the magical, swooping sounds he was hearing. Rennie and the girl led the other couples in a circle that could have been from a castle ballroom. Each man lured his partner into the circle and bowed before joining the spinning wheel of dancers, then off they would whirl. It made David slightly dizzy just to keep track of the two lead dancers in all the melee of colors and flashing combinations of male-to-female bodies.

But Rennie and the girl would always stand out, even in a crowd of advanced dancers like this. Their dancing ability set them apart, of course, but their sheer love of the dance made them sparkle like finely-cut gems among common pebbles. They complimented each other in almost every way; she was fair and he was dark, she was tiny and he was tall, she looked as sweet as sugar and he looked as dangerous as dynamite.

The waltzing wheel quickly collapsed on itself on the final beats of the music, forming a double line facing forward, ladies in front and gentlemen backing them up, but still holding them by one hand. Together they looked out on what would be the audience, took one step, then another, and the girls sank to the floor in a graceful curtsey as the men made a formal bow. Their sole audience member up in the tree was guessing it would be a showstopper for the year-end benefit performance when all the women would probably be wearing ballgowns and the men would be in white tie and tails.

The year-end dance performance. Gordie had invited him to go. They would cheer on his sister, Luisa. Yes, he'd never been to a dance concert before. It might be interesting. It wasn't that he wanted to see Rennie and the girl dancing together. He'd convinced himself that it wasn't the dancers themselves he was interested in, only that the combination of music and graceful movement seemed to soothe him like nothing else. If anyone had told him before this that watching classes of dancers, or one particular dancer, would have a calming effect on him, he would have laughed.

Walking on to the Chemistry building he went over in his mind how often he'd seen the girl lately. Now that he knew what to look for it seemed he was seeing her everywhere. She had an extra-thick head of long, wavy, ash blonde hair and outside of class she usually had it flowing free. He liked it that way. In class it usually had to be pinned up.

Up close she was as lovely as he'd imagined, with pouty lips that flashed in machine-gun bursts of smiles, giggles, and laughter. Everywhere she went, people gathered around her. If he saw her in the student union when he was getting lunch, she'd be out in the courtyard break-dancing with the black chicks. If he passed an early art class set up for outdoor sketches, all the students had their easels set up around hers and were constantly commenting on her work. He'd never seen a girl so popular. But she never hung around the science wing.

Today he entered the lab through the rear door. "We have to set up everything there is to set up," Gordie informed him when he'd gotten his lab coat on. "Robert's orders."

"When did this happen?" David was puzzled. The first day of a beginning chemistry class didn't demand any actual lab work, let alone setting up an entire lab.

"Our mighty leader had an inspiration this morning; dazzle them with firepower. Set up the lab and take their collective breaths away, which of course means you and I get to set it up and take it back down again. I'll have to leave for a class here in a minute, Mark will come in to help for a while but he'll have to leave, too. Then it's just you to run the class until Robert gets here. I'll beat it back as soon as I can after class, but at least nothing needs to be washed. Robert will demand they be at least wiped down, though.

David was aware of their professor's ultra-neat ways and groaned a little inside, but began retrieving test tubes he'd used the night before from the adjoining secondary lab. Students were already arriving.

He was standing at the sink rinsing a test tube when he looked out the window and saw them; Rennie, Luisa and two of the other dancers with the girl were coming out of the dance building and walking to the bridge. She had let her hair down and the sun was shining through it making it glow like liquid gold. Her ballet skirt had been replaced with a muslin tie-dyed knee length wrap that matched her leotard exactly, and her feet were bare.

All of a sudden Rennie called their attention to a spot on the stream half-way to the Chemistry building, a place where sanitation workers had found a need to remove a section of fence on each side of the stream to clear away some kind of hazardous material. From where they were standing it looked like a short space from one side to the other, maybe four feet, but David could see from his higher angle how deceptive that was. What looked like solid ground on their side was really just loose clods of dirt with no support underneath. With a start he realized they were daring the girl to jump it.

"NO!" Gripping the test tube in his right hand, he tried to beat on the window with his left to get their attention, yelling "NO!" although he knew with the soundproof windows they couldn't hear him and he was up too high for them to notice. All their attention was on the lovely young girl, who pirouetted around and eyed the gulf while her friends made little signs with their hands, obviously reminding her of the many jumps she'd made in class much longer than this.

Too easily she gave in. David ached to see her hand over books, purse and the sandals she was carrying to Luisa, stretch her feet, and begin to run down the short length of slope. As she gathered speed he clenched his fists and watched in fear as she neared the edge, then...

Then she was in the air. *How did she do it?* David wondered. Below her the section of fragile earth was collapsing into the streambed and her friends gasped to see how close she'd come to disaster.

At the apex of her leap she pulled her upper torso backwards so she was arched up to the sun, her hair flying behind her, the back leg slightly bent and the front leg straight as an arrow. Her arms were lifted up to the sky and he could see her laugh with joy.

Then she was safely down, and two steps brought her into the arms of a shocked security guard. Her friends were hurrying down to help her and David heard a noise behind him. Turning his head, he realized Mark had stood in the doorway for the entire scene, and was now wearing an expression as dazed as his own.

Trying to regain his focus, David asked, "And what was *that*?"

Mark looked at him with a look almost of pity and said, "*That*, my friend, was Gelsy," and he was gone.

Gelsy?

He looked down at his hand. The test tube was crushed and blood oozed from several small cuts on his hand into the sink.

"Damn!" he thought, as turned the water on to wash out the glass.

-7-

Robert hadn't come in yet, but David wasn't surprised. He'd been expecting to take roll and get the class settled in on his own; Robert's "baptism by fire."

In as few words as possible he gave his name, position, explained he's been an army drill sergeant (Robert had insisted he do that) and told them all seating was final. Beginning with the seat closest to the lectern he began taking names and drawing up the seating chart Robert wanted.

It was going well. His cool demeanor, height, and background in the army, all made these first-year students decide not to play games with this particular TA. He had nearly completed the list when he realized the door had quietly opened and closed, and there was a new student in the room.

No, not a new student, a new presence. Standing nearly on the tips of her bare feet and looking over the heads of the people seated in the room was… *the girl.* She held her notebooks clutched to her chest, and her long hair swayed as she scanned one side of the room to the other. Finally she was looking directly into David's eyes. He immediately felt like he was being cut down by enemy fire, and reacted almost in pain.

"What are you doing, standing there like that?" His tone was rougher than he expected.

Her eyes widened, and he could see their color now. They were hazel, or were they green? They seemed almost iridescent.

"What is your name?"

"Grandwood." Her voice had a slight accent.

He forced his attention back to the roll sheet, to the *G*s. "Yes, 'Grandwood, Gah-zall."

Some in the class tittered and she put her chin up a little to correct him. "Giselle, *Giselle Marie!*"

He knew he was flushing but couldn't help it. "Hmm, yes. Please sit down, Ms. Grandwood."

Like a stone she dropped to the floor, crossed her legs, and piled her belongings on her lap. He looked at her in astonishment. "I meant, *at a seat*, Miss Grandwood!"

"There *aren't any!*" she replied, defiantly.

He looked around the room again and realized… she was right. Every seat was taken. But the roll sheet showed they had exactly the correct number of students this room would hold. What had happened?

It was too late now, Robert was entering through the rear door in a delightful mood that David realized would soon turn to rage over the fact that the new TA had not made sure ahead of time there were enough desks for the number of students enrolled in the class.

"Oh my, look at this," Robert chirped, "My class is all seated and the lab is ready to go. How wonderful it is to have a dependable TA," he smiled at David, who just looked at him with a face frozen in shame. Robert walked around the side of the class. "I can see we're starting the day on a…," then he saw the forlorn little dancer seated on the floor in front of him, "*Mon dieu!*"

This was not the reaction David expected, but he tried to stammer something about seating. No one was listening. Everyone was watching the drama unfolding.

"*Mon DIEU!*" Robert had exclaimed again, dropping his briefcase and pounding his head against the whiteboard, quite theatrically.

"*Bon jour*, Buba," said the girl, rather arrogantly.

"Giselle Marie Grandwood, what are you doing here? In *MY CLASS*? On *MY FLOOR*??!"

"This was the *only* beginning science class I could fit into my schedule and you know I'm required to have one this quarter. And I'm on your floor because there aren't enough seats and that one *there* told me to sit *down*!" She pouted and pointed at David, who now realized the slight accent she had was probably French.

Robert let out a long, dramatic sigh, looked at David and winked, then motioned him over.

Walking over to the girl he scooped her up in his arms and presented her to David like a child.

"This, David, is my god-daughter, Gelsy. But don't think that because I'm her god-father she has any knowledge of science; her entire left brain is taken up with a storage of tutus and toe-shoes. If you and I can whip her through a required science class with at least a 'C,' her parents – who are both on our faculty - will be ever-so-grateful."

With that he dumped the girl into David's arms and began to drag his own heavy wooden chair from behind his desk.

To be standing in front of his class, holding this other-worldly creature in his arms so quickly, was one of the worse moments of David's life. He couldn't bring himself to look at her, but he didn't know where else to look. It didn't help that Robert continued as he brought a small writing stand around to where he'd placed the chair, "Now, you promise to obey David, Gelsy. He's brilliant and will probably win a Nobel someday."

David flushed an even deeper shade, then all color drained from his face as the girl leaned slightly closer to him and announced, "But... he smokes, Buba!" Putting her dainty little nose in the air, she jumped down.

"Ah, yes. He was in the army. They practically require you to smoke, *mon infant*. But not to worry, we will keep him

24

so busy in the lab he will have no time for it and would soon give it up anyway. A good scientist needs his sense of smell." He seated her at her new place and put one hand firmly on her head. Looking with great love into her eyes he said, "Now, stay right there and be silent in any language you choose."

"*Oui*, Buba!" she replied, and kissed his hand.

Robert indicated David should stand behind the desk while he himself took the lectern, rubbing his hands with glee. "Now, class, let's talk about science. I realize not one of you is here because you have a deep love of chemistry. If you were, you'd be majoring in the subject. So you may wonder why I choose each year to teach one entry level class like this. Well, it is precisely because all of you come here with no set ideas, no preconceived notions about biochemistry. Each of you has a different way of looking at my great love that adds something to the way I see it. Because of you I have a chance to see all my tired, old theories through new eyes, and I revel in it!"

David was entranced. He had them all, Gelsy included, in the palm of his hand. Because he did love the subject matter, he'd make it interesting for them, and he'd respect their contributions. David made a mental note to always include his students in each class, not just teach down to them as so many had to him.

"And you'll notice the full beauty of a completely prepared lab behind you," Robert continued now. "This is due to the hard work of David and his assistants. I wanted you to see how exciting it can look when it is ready to go for your Thursday classes so you'll look forward to them instead of dreading them. And you're so lucky today, because David and his assistants will also put it all away! From now on, it will be your responsibility to set up and clean up what you need; David will be here only to assist." (At this Gelsy flashed him a smile.) And he has orders to check everything; I like my equipment clean!"

Robert continued speaking of the excitement of chemistry for another fifteen minutes but he could have held them there for an hour, easily. He was a marvelous speaker and even Gelsy, who must have heard him speak on the subject many times, was as enthralled as everyone else. David was glad to see that she obviously had great love and admiration for her god-father. Then he nearly choked when he remembered, *But she thinks you stink*!

The speech ended and Gelsy jumped up to give Robert a standing ovation, which the rest of the class joined in on before grabbing their books to fly off for their next classes or, more likely, lunch. Robert took advantage of Gelsy's standing to retrieve his chair and writing table, handing them off to David who replaced them behind the huge, oaken desk.

"Ah, Buba, *c'est magnifique*!"

Robert kissed her forehead, but just then a pair of hands slipped around the girl's head, covering her eyes and Robert took the chance to escape and talk to other students.

"Guess who?" Gordie had crept up on her.

"Oh, too easy, *amigo*," and in a torrent of Spanish they skipped away to the lab.

"Be silent in any language you choose," Robert had said. David shook his head and followed them.

Gordie had lifted Gelsy up onto one of the unused lab tables and was already beginning the process of deconstruction. "OK, give, *chica*. I want it all. Oh, David, we've got to at least look like we're dusting or Robert will be down on us for leaving fingerprints. Start at the beginning, Gelsy. Why are you here?"

That question took David by surprise. Why was she here? Robert was her god-father, her parents were both on faculty, why *wouldn't* she be here?

"You mean, like everybody else and their Aunt Maude, why am I not still in New York?"

Gordie stopped with the test tubes and walked over to her. Besides being old friends, it was immediately clear to David that Gordie adored this girl.

"I mean, *chica*, that you had a full scholarship with ABT. That I heard you danced brilliantly with the student company all summer, and that the greatest male dancer of the century had you pegged as his future partner."

Here the girl's head dropped, almost in shame, David thought. Some of this was beginning to make sense.

"Don't be like everyone else, Gordie. Try to understand me. You're one of the few who can. If I try to tell them the real reason they misunderstand and gossip."

Gordie flushed. "You know I'll do my best, Gelsy."

"Ok Gordie. I came back because I had to. I couldn't stay away any longer."

"You were homesick, honey? You're only eighteen, it's understandable."

"And how many times have I studied away from home? I know homesickness. This was not it."

"You weren't running away from anything, were you, honey?"

"No, and don't go making a gossip item out of it, that I was afraid of Naj and his reputation with the women. There were other places I could have gone."

"New York City Ballet offered you a place, too, didn't they, Gelsy?"

She sat up. "How do you know this?! Oh, of course, your oldest sister, Victoria. She should be more careful, Gordie. Tell her so. She has her job as a costumer to protect. New York is horrible about people who tell tales out of school."

"I'll tell her. But you have to admit, to those of us who admire you and have for years thought the world should be at your feet, coming back to do a freshman year of college was a… OK, I won't say disappointment, but certainly a huge surprise. It looked like you had it all, Gelsy."

She was silent, twisting the fabric of her skirt. David found himself aching for her to speak again; not only to know the answers but just to hear her voice.

"I thought I had to choose between ABT and NYCB. I admire them both, and I've danced in both their summer programs. I knew it would be a hard decision. What I didn't know was that when I went to make it, there was no decision at all. I was coming home and going to school. That was it. There was no alternative. It wasn't my parents or fear of failing or any of the things people keep saying. I wish I could tell you what it was. I just knew my life was here, not in New York." She looked up with teary eyes. "And now you must let me go get something to eat so I can make it to my next class."

Swinging herself off the table, she stopped and turned around. "David, I want to apologize for mentioning the fact you smoke in front of the class. That was extremely disrespectful of me. I'm so sorry."

David was glad his back was turned. He continued wiping down a test tube and said, "It's really OK because I've been thinking about what Robert told you. That I'll be too busy in the lab to smoke much now, anyway. And that a scientist needs his sense of smell."

Gelsy brightened. "So you will stop?!"

Her eagerness surprised him. He put the test tube away and turned to her. "Yes, I will."

"When?" She was insistent.

David considered the matter. "Now, I guess."

She held out her little hand with the long, slender fingers. "Then give them to me."

"Give you… what?"

"The cigarettes in your shirt pocket. Give them to me."

David reached past his lab coat, into the pocket of his white shirt and retrieved the half-empty pack. He looked at it for a moment, then put it in her hand. Triumphantly her fingers closed on it as her body lifted straight up into the air. Holding the pack of cigarettes overhead, she beat her bare feet in the air and cried out, '*c'est magnifique!*"

Zipping them into her backpack, she grabbed her belongings and started for the door.

"Wait, Gelsy," Gordie said, "What are you going to *do* with that damn pack of cigarettes, anyway?"

"My next class is art," she giggled. "I will make a montage of them. They will do no harm to anyone there!" And then she was gone. Mark had to jump out of her way, she barely had time to touch his shoulder before flying.

As he came in the room it occurred to David they all stood in the same place for a moment, as if hoping she'd come back.

-8-

"So why does she call him "Buba?" David had been grilling Gordie without realizing it for nearly twenty minutes as they laid out the lab for the next day.

"When she was a little girl she couldn't say *Robert*, and it came out 'Buba.' So that's what it's been ever since." Gordie was gratified to have one area of expertise higher than his new TA's.

"She speaks Spanish and French?"

"French because Adele, true Parisian that she is, insisted that she be born in Paris so she could have a double-citizenship passport. Plus she spent a summer on her own studying at the Paris Opera ballet when she was fifteen. Spanish, because she grew up with my family, of course. And then there's Russian, from the summer sessions she spent at sixteen and seventeen with the Kirov."

"So she speaks, what? Four languages?!"

"Five. Her Italian is pretty good, too. She took classes in Milan as a child."

David was overwhelmed. He couldn't help but wonder what language she dreamed in. As if guessing, Gordie said, "She considers French her native language."

French. And he didn't know a damned word of French.

The quarter continued. A routine formed with the classes and hours of research in Robert's special labs. In between, David formed the habit of taking a sandwich up to his nest by the dance room for lunch whenever he knew Gelsy had a class. That he cared about her didn't occur to him, only that watching her dance calmed him when the stress of research gone wrong or disruptive students became too much for him to handle. He was still seeing his therapist one hour a week for his PTSD but one hour was hardly enough, and he refused to take medication.

When David had first arrived, Robert had invited him to dinner with some friends. David, thinking of a semi-formal dinner in the company of professors and their families, was horrified and begged off with excuses. Robert allowed it, but continued to ask and gradually it dawned on David that the "friends" Robert was referring to were Gelsy and her parents, Donald and Adele Grandwood.

Donald Grandwood was head of the music department, well-known in the field of music anthropology and just a "heck of a nice guy," according to Gordie, who had known the family all his life. "My mom was one of their 'helpers,' they wouldn't have 'maids,' back when Gelsy was little, so we all played together. Rennie's mom worked for them part-time, too, but she was driving their car the day some kid running a red light crashed into her and killed her. Donald and Adele did everything for Rennie and his two sisters; paid for their dance classes, saw they got college scholarships, everything. When Rennie wanted to compete in some fancy ballet tournament in Milan last year, Donald paid for both of them to go so Gelsy could be his partner. That's why Rennie won, if you ask me. But he goes around with his chest puffed out because he was Best New Male Dancer of the Year."

"They why isn't *he* in New York?" David wanted to know.

"He was!" Gordie was almost white with rage. "When he found out Gelsy was set on coming back he begged Donald to get him a dance scholarship so he could come back, too. Personally, I think that's the last thing Gelsy wanted, but he's using it now like 'the two of them' decided to come back 'together." Gordie growled. "He keeps trying to get himself invited over to their house for the weekly Friday dinner, but she just manages to let it roll off her back."

"What Friday night dinner?"

"Oh, it's called the 'hoot' and it's been going on for years. Chaveral goes over, they all eat, drink wine, sing and have a get-down party."

"Why a 'hoot?'"

For 'hootenanny.' Like in the early 1960s, you know? Bob Dylan, the Kingston Trio, Joan Baez, all that crowd. Donald and Chaveral were two shaggy college kids with guitars, busking their way around Europe when they met Adele in Paris and they've all been together ever since."

David looked like he'd been hit with a baseball bat. "Robert... plays a guitar... and *sings*?? No way!"

Gordie grinned. "Way, man, *WAY*. And depending on whether or not he's been hitting the bourbon, you can even hear some of the best blues you'll hear this side of New Orleans."

-9-

It was later on that morning when Gelsy poked her head in the lab. Surprised, David turned to her and blurted out, "I'm the only one here, Gelsy. Robert and Gordie went to lunch together."

"That's OK, Davey, it's you I came to see" and she glided into the room like a shadow.

Davey? Where had that come from?!

"It's about the hoot tonight, Davey."

"The hoot… yeah, Gordie was trying to explain it to me. Sounds interesting."

"Well, Buba would really like for you to come and I think he's a little disappointed that you always turn him down, but I got to thinking it might be because I'm in your class. Is that it, Davey?" And here she looked up at him with those eyes of indescribable color.

"Umm, that might be a reason. Also because I don't really have anything nice to wear..."

"We wear jeans and tee-shirts!"

"OK, that solves that. Also because I'm not used to being around people, Gelsy. I did three tours of duty in Afghanistan and came back with post-traumatic shock syndrome disorder. I stress out easily in new situations."

"But Davey, if you are going to be a teacher, a professor… if you are going to give lectures and attend seminars, shouldn't you be trying to make yourself learn to accept new people and new situations? Especially small, friendly groups like ours with food, wine, and music?"

She had him there. "And also, you're my student, Gelsy."

"But I'm also Buba's student, and he comes. The quarter will be over before long and you would come then? Why deprive yourself these weeks when the weather is so nice to sit outside? I will make no trouble and Gordie can be the one to mentor me in lab. You don't even need to speak to me if you don't want to."

He was caught. He had to admit, she was good. "OK, Gelsy, I'll be there tonight."

She brightened up so quickly it made his heart stop, but then she said, "Buba will be so pleased. He was afraid you were not liking his company. I will tell him to pick you up at the dorm at five-thirty, is that OK?"

"That will be fine."

"Remember, it's a hoot. Jeans and tee-shirts only."

"I'll remember."

And she was gone. But he'd be spending the evening in her company. What would that be like? Jeans and tee-shirts. Did she realize his only tee-shirts were frayed army-issue? OK, he figured, I just have enough time to buy a school tee-shirt at the student union.

-10-

Driving up to the dorm that night, Robert was surprised to find a tall, handsome man in a long-sleeved, green-and-gold UCSM-logo tee-shirt waiting for him. "I swear, David, you look five years younger! Suddenly you really look like a college student instead of a professor-in-training."

"Well, I'm not sure if that's a compliment, Robert, seeing as how I've seen my twenty-seventh birthday come and go this month. I'm so much older than most of the students I live with here at the dorm."

Robert was startled. "This month, oh Lord, I missed your birthday! It was last week, wasn't it?"

Now David was surprised. "That's right. How did you know? I didn't think anybody but the army knew."

"And the university, don't forget! It's printed on all your formal documents. I saw it once and meant to make a note of it. That damn conference call to Buenos Aires fell on the same day, didn't it? Crap, I was going to take you out to lunch." Robert looked totally chagrined.

"Robert, it's enough to know you even thought of me," David said with appreciation, and they were silent the rest of the short trip.

As they pulled into the circular driveway, piano music drifted out to greet them. David got out of the car and looked through an open dormer window to see Gelsy seated at a grand piano. "I didn't know she played," was all he could think of to say.

"Her father a music professor?" Robert snorted. "She's been playing concertos since she was six!" He went around to the front door but turned back. David was in the same place, staring through the window at the girl whose hair was glowing from the light on a piano stand, playing the *Moonlight Sonata*.

Robert smiled and waved him over. "Hey, you can hear better from inside."

David snapped to attention and followed him sheepishly through the door, then down a few steps into a sunken living room. Gelsy immediately switched to a few chords of "When the Saints Come Marching In" which seemed to be the cue for a tall, handsome blonde man and his tiny, very French-looking wife to appear on the opposite stairway.

"We're just setting up the food, *mon cherie*, but introduce us to your protégé first!" said the little lady who could be no one but Gelsy's mother. Her accent, hair, devastating beauty all marked her as such.

"Donald and Adele, I am so pleased to present David Collins to you, and so horrified that I forgot last week was his birthday. May we make it up to him tonight?"

Cries of welcome were mixed with congratulations and sorrow over the birthday neglect. Promises of a night to remember were made and David was so flushed with all their attention, he didn't know what to say or where to look. Gelsy, suddenly remembering his PTSD, took his arm and said, "Let me show David the patio and pool while you three finish setting out the dinner. He's not used to being fawned over like this."

And off she led him, through the sliding glass patio doors and out onto a lanai covered with thatch but open to the sky farther on. A long, low table was surrounded by soft, overstuffed pieces of furniture that looked like they were bought at Salvation Army and set up to be jumped on and have chlorine dripped on them. David liked that. It looked comfortable. There was even a "unisex restroom" sign on the bathroom door, so you knew exactly where to go if you felt nature call. It all looked very homey.

"You see," Gelsy said, "It really is a 'family night' here. The food is set up and you help yourself, then we come out to the patio for music and wine and to tell old, old stories." She giggled and said, "Papa and Buba will be so happy to have a new audience member for their stories, Davey!" as she led him back inside for dinner.

-11-

Gelsy hadn't lied, the food was served smorgasbord-style and it was delicious. A light, white wine was poured along with lemonade and water, and David thought he'd never eaten anything as good as Adele's croissants. When he told her he could have made his meal on them and been happy, she was overjoyed. A true daughter of Paris, she considered pastry to be the absolute pinnacle of culinary skills.

The one thorn in his side was the way they'd keep slipping into French. All four spoke it fluently and obviously used it whenever the subject seemed to call for a Parisian point of view, but Gelsy would gently call them back with, "Remember, Davey doesn't speak French."

"You never took French in school, David?" Donald asked.

"No, sir. I took German in college because that's what the science books in my major seemed to be in, and also in the army we'd get shipped from Afghanistan to Hamburg for R&R. Now my German is pretty decent… but no French."

"Well, we just happen to have one of the top professors of French right here at the table," and Donald made a low bow in the direction of his wife. "So tell me, my dear, how can we remedy this situation so David can attend the next Paris Conference with Robbie?"

Robert nearly tipped over his chair. "Donnie, how bright of you! Yes, I would want very much to have his help at the conference. Let's sign him up for French lessons, as if he hasn't got enough to do already!"

Adele sat at the foot of the table, with her hands crossed in front of her, listening to the three men and said, "Poor David does have too much to do for regular classes. But I have some audio lessons he can listen to while he brushes his teeth, does his laundry or even sleeps. And when he is here, we can each help him with his vocabulary. Just here at the table, we can start by making him ask for a glass of water or a napkin in French."

Donald looked at her as though he'd married an angel, which he had, and pronounced, "That is obviously the best solution. Don't make it a chore for David, just have him over every week and have him listen to us. We'll drum it into his head soon enough."

Every week? They were going to have him back every week? David felt like his breath had been taken away for a minute. Could they really want his company that much?

"Splendid, Donnie! I love the idea of having fresh ears for all our tired, old tales and ditties! David, you wouldn't believe the amount of material we have stored up from our days on the road as a couple of long-haired troubadours. You're looking at a couple of grey-bearded, old professors who had a hard time just growing a few chin-whiskers back when Adele met us! But how we loved our music, didn't we, Donnie? We'd sing in train terminals, bus stations, town squares, anyplace they'd let us put a guitar case down to collect a few dollars. And we'd sing all the great songs from America. Speaking of which, is everyone ready to move out to the patio?"

-12-

Once settled out on the patio with an amazing variety of musical instruments, Robert called for the "guest of honor" to choose the first song. It took a minute before David realized they were referring to him, but he gamely replied he wanted to hear something from their old days of traveling around Europe. With a sparkle in his eye, Robert winked at Donald and whispered, "Greenback Dollar," and they were off like a runaway train.

If David hadn't seen it, he never would have believed it. Two distinguished university professors (backed on guitar by a ballerina) howling with great abandon about how they didn't give a damn about a greenback dollar! The Kingston Trio would have been hard-pressed to do better.

David hadn't even finished applauding when Adele appeared at the patio doors to begin a triumphant march through the lanai bearing a magnificent frosted cake glowing with candles.

"A birthday cake," David thought. "How did they get a birthday cake so fast?"

"Mama made it for you." Gelsy had appeared at his elbow. "That's why I had to bring you out to show you the patio when you first came so she could whip it up and get it in the oven. And she frosted it while Papa and Buba were singing."

David didn't know what to say or do. Donald was taking photos and telling his wife what a genius she was while Robert and Gelsy called him the "birthday boy", and here he stood -- unable to open his mouth.

"I hope you like it, Davey," Adele said. (He noticed she had slipped into calling him "Davey" now, as Gelsy did.) I didn't know what kind you like, so I made the bottom chocolate and the top banana cream. The frosting is a combination of both.

The cake indeed had two layers, the bottom being slightly larger to hold the twenty-seven flickering candles. The top was round and frosted in yellow, with sliced bananas marching around the base. On the top, in chocolate letters, was simply written, "David."

"Blow out the candles, Davey!" Gelsy looked like she was ready to jump up and down.

"Don't forget to make a wish!"

"Blow out the candles? Do I have to?" David enjoyed just looking at it. "I've never had a birthday cake before."

He wasn't expecting the reaction that last sentence received, and it was lucky he was so engrossed in looking at the cake itself he didn't notice. Donald and Robert looked like they'd been hit by a truck, Adele went white and Gelsy turned away, trying not to cry.

Robert quickly picked up the conversation, "No, it's house rules, you gotta blow out the candles and make your wish for the year. You'll get another one next year and we took pictures of this one, so go ahead – make a wish and *blow!*"

David immediately leaned over the cake, taking a deep breath and blowing each candle out in turn. Standing back up again, everyone congratulated him as if he'd just run a marathon while Adele ran for the plates.

It was fantastic; how could it not be? Adele made it. Sitting out there, slowly eating his piece of cake he realized Gelsy was picking up her guitar. Strumming softly, she began to sing "Blue Bayou." Looking out to the blue lights encircling the swimming pool and the stars overhead, David couldn't believe this was all now part of *his* world.

-13-

And so another constant was added to his way of life. In addition to his classes, research, study, grading papers (although Gordie did most of that), and having lunch in his nest while watching one of Gelsy's dance classes, David found himself walking around the campus whispering French words and trying to prepare himself for that Friday's hoot. Mark and Gordie would watch in stark envy as he walked out the door every week to meet Robert's car. ("We hate you," seemed to be their standard phrase.) They had been on hand that first Friday night to help him polish off the remainder of the birthday cake Adele had sent home with him. Life should have been good.

So why wasn't it? Why was he starting to feel edgy again? Was it because the quarter was almost over and he had mid-terms – both in his own classes and in the one he assisted – to worry about? Was it the weather turning cooler? Gelsy was wearing sweaters out on the patio and soon it would be too cold to go out there. And when the quarter was over there would be no reason for Gelsy to come around the Chemistry department, certainly not three times a week like she did now. Now he could be sure to see and talk to her on Mondays, Tuesdays and Thursdays, then at the hoot on Friday nights. In between he could watch her dance every weekday. Weekends were getting bad. He forced himself to spend every minute studying or working with Robert to keep his mind occupied until Monday morning came again.

Gelsy, always *Gelsy*. He was getting as bad as Gordie, Mark or any number of the guys in the dorm who'd hang out in the lobby and moon openly about being "madly in love" with Gelsy Grandwood. David heard stories that at the frat houses some of the biggest studs on campus put up a betting pool to see which among them would get a date with her. Not even get to first base with her, mind you, just snag a date to the movies. The captain of the football team, the kid from the wealthiest family, the Senator's son… they all struck out.

But David wasn't joining their pool. He'd come for a doctoral program and a chance at some real research and that was going to be his focus. Women were never a distraction for him. The ones he'd seen on the streets and in the army left him with little desire to spend more than a certain amount of time with them. Never really having a mother, no sisters or contact with women in early years left him emotionally leery of their sex. Gelsy and Adele were the only two he could stand to talk to for more than a few minutes at a time.

But there was this feeling eating at him, making him want to do things again. He told his therapist, "OK, I know masturbation is a natural male thing but I really try to keep it down just because it can take me over, like an addiction. Then I want to start looking for a hooker, like I did in the army – but I promised myself I'm not doing that again because it always left me feeling so lousy. And it took all my money."

His therapist reminded him that these were all rules he was making for himself, based on observations he'd made… on himself.

"You're a scientist through and through, David. You are trying to solve a problem here. Maybe you need to think outside the box for once." The ex-marine was trying to be kind.

"Could you be a little more specific?"

The man shifted uneasily in his chair. "I don't think I should be spelling anything out for you if you seem determined not to see it on your own. I'm just worried that the frustration of not dealing properly with it may make you fall back on some old habits. Promise me you'll call me if that happens."

Old habits. Which "old habits" was the jarhead talking about?

-14-

The morning had dawned and David woke up from a nightmare. Was it the war? No, he couldn't remember the sound of explosions… with war dreams he always heard explosions. Especially the one that… no, don't go there, he thought.

He sat up. Why was he soaking wet? Then he realized his pillow was in the middle of the bed, and it was wet. Closing his eyes, he remembered kissing a girl with long, soft hair. A girl who called him, "Davey." He blinked his eyes and slapped himself, hard. "This has got to stop," he thought. "I'm going crazy!"

For the first time, he bypassed the dance building. There was another route to the Chemistry building but he'd never taken it – it was longer and went by the sports areas. Today he made that trip and tried to make himself pretend an interest in the young athletes warming up for their track and field work.

There were young women practicing jumping hurdles, but they seemed clumsy compared to a dancer clearing the studio in great leaps. The runners were fast but looked awkward next to the grace of a ballerina in her pointe shoes, skimming the floor. Why was he even making comparisons like that?

He walked on. This route took twice as long as the usual walk and next took him by the art department. Gelsy came here often, both to take classes and to model. The life studies classes all vied to have her pose for their students; she could stand in any position completely still for hours. Wait, he was doing it again. He was thinking about her.

Back at the lab David thought about what his therapist had said, but trying to untangle it all made his head ache.

Every sound seemed magnified. A tiny knock at the door sounded like thunder, tearing his raw nerves apart. "What is it?" He snapped, as Gelsy smilingly waltzed into the room.

"Davey, I'm through with lab and I've cleaned up everything. Would you like to have lunch with me?" she said, pirouetting neatly into a flawless fifth position.

Now she stood there, smiling, dressed in her trademark paper-thin jeans and skintight black turtleneck sweater with the gold cross hanging from her neck. Obviously she'd had a good morning class, because she always waltzed when she'd had a particularly good morning class.

"Too much information," David thought to himself. "I'm starting to know her too well, and like her too much."

Out loud he barked, "No, Gelsy, it is not *appropriate* for us to go out to lunch together. It is not even *appropriate* for you to come in here and be alone with me. None of the other students would be so familiar."

He refocused his microscope and then glanced up just in time to see her lovely face turn white before she disappeared out the door.

-15-

Where was the phone number? It was Friday and he'd already decided to make some excuse to skip the hoot tonight. Since he'd thrown Gelsy out of the lab yesterday he hadn't been by to watch her dance or done much besides search for the number Jensen had given him just before he left Carmichael.

"I'm not going to be needing this down there," David had said to Jensen at first.

"Hang on to it in case something happens, and the gun, too. You never know. SoCal is tricky."

Well, he'd found that out, but not quite in the way Jensen meant. The gun he finally found shoved into a big plastic jar that used to hold salted nuts, and amazingly, the slip of paper was with it.

Five minutes later David was off on a cross-campus bus for the southernmost tip of the university. (He chose this over walking so he wouldn't be tempted to stop and watch any dance classes on the way.) When he reached the symbolic gates he went past them and on to the first block of businesses beyond that existed solely for students; a pizza parlor, ice-cream shop, trendy clothes store, beer and pool hall, movie theater, and bookstore.

He went into the pizza parlor and asked to speak to "Antonio from upstate." A stocky, mean-looking Italian came out of the kitchen and sized him up. "Who told you to ask for me like that?" he snapped.

"A guy I knew in Carmichael, named Jensen. He said you'd point out another guy to me. Somebody named 'T-Bone Boy.' Ring any bells?"

Antonio gave him another look up and down, then picked up a phone and dialed a number.

The conversation was strange; no "Hello" or exchange of names, just "Yeah, that's him," and "Jensen, upstate. Useta be in the army wit' me." When he hung up, he turned David by the shoulder to look out the window, across the street to the beer & pool hall. Standing in the window was a black man in a dark-blue suit who nodded and walked in back.

By the time David got over to the pool hall, two tough kids in hoodies had positioned themselves at the door. They 'accidently on purpose' bumped into him on their way out, then turned and gave a sign to someone that he was carrying a gun in the back of his waistband, under his windbreaker. The news didn't seem to alarm anyone, more likely to soothe them, David thought. If he was packing, it put him more in their social circle.

The man in the blue suit waved him over to a table. "Beer?"

"No thanks. Drank too much of that in the army." The man called for two Scotch on the rocks and David didn't argue. By this time it was sounding good.

"So you work over on campus?" The man was obviously trying to decode David by his age, bearing, vocabulary, clothing and anything else he could get a handle on.

"Graduate student, by way of the military." David took the first sip of Scotch and for once welcomed the heat. "Midterms coming up and I'm thinking I may need a little help to make it through."

"You were thinking of…"

"H if I can get it."

"With me, you can, and good stuff, too. How much?"

"Not much. Just to get me through. I don't want to get started again."

The man in the suit smiled like he'd heard this one before, but said only, "As a new client, I'm going to give you a freebie. You like it, you come back to me and we talk business. You're up in that new north dorm, aren't you?" (How did he know that?) "Well, if you like it maybe you can let some of those people know about my services."

With that he pulled a cheap, folded paper envelope from his pocket and slid it across the table to David, who took it, glanced inside just to see the whitish powder in a glassine packet, then slipped it into his inner jacket pocket. Immediately he wanted to be out of that pool hall, but it would be rude not to finish the drink. As calmly as possible he told the man a little (as little as possible) about himself and how he came to be in SoCal, drank the rest of the Scotch, excused himself and left to find a cross-campus bus to the student union.

-16-

He still had to get lunch. Just knowing he had the drug in his pocket made him feel less edgy, so he might as well eat and stick as much as possible to the day's routine. Heading back he thought he passed the two young men in sweatshirts who had bumped into him in the pool hall. Were they following him? No, that's crazy. Of course they'd be students here, too. He tried to shake the feeling that he was being followed. What if drug enforcement agents had the pool hall staked out? What if he got caught on campus with drugs and a loaded gun? With his record, even Robert couldn't save him.

By now he was starting to sweat a little. He took his lunch and headed for someplace he could at least felt safe -- his nest outside the dance room window. Before he dropped from the bridge he carefully checked each pathway to make sure no one could see him, and in ten seconds he was sitting in the tree.

It was early. The beginning ballet was still in session, which meant the advanced dancers for the next class would be stretching out in the hallways. What was the next class at this time on Fridays? This wasn't his usual time and he couldn't remember. Just don't let it be a class with Rennie and Gelsy together, he thought. Anything but that.

Last night Gordie had confided something to him that had just about made his head spin and had a lot to do with today's edginess. It seemed that Rennie, growing desperate by Gelsy's coolness to him, had concocted a story he was letting only a few, select male friends in on.

In his version of their New York summer, Gelsy came over to see his apartment (which he neglected to mention he shared with three other guys) and ended up spending the night. Rennie blamed the bottle of strong wine he'd served for dinner and castigated himself for not being more of a gentleman, but there it was… the real reason Gelsy had run back home. But no matter, she 'belonged' to *him* now, and everyone must understand his feelings for her.

Luckily one of the boys had a sister, who, as with Gordie and Luisa, he told everything to. She promptly told Luisa who told Gordie who told Gelsy. Looking back, David realized when Gelsy asked him to have lunch with her, she was really asking him to make a statement that she was not Rennie's property. It had all suddenly made him sick.

The doors were opening now, and the advanced ballet *pas de deux* class entered. Well, wasn't that just what he needed to see? A class where Rennie and Gelsy did nothing but dance together. He'd finish his lunch and be on his way as quickly as possible.

Gelsy looked like a dancer from an old Technicolor movie today, in a two-piece indigo dance trunk and bra set with a purple sash around her waist and a matching headband. Even her legwarmers were lavender. David wouldn't have been surprised if Gene Kelly had appeared to lift her in his arms and twirl her off into a panoramic set, she looked so adorable. Only the sad expression on her face clashed with the outfit. Gelsy looked tired, as if she hadn't been getting enough sleep. And thinner, too. David sat up and took notice. "She's lost weight!"

By now the couples had warmed up and were taking their starting positions. Rennie and Gelsy were placed in front to lead the others and David was able to get a better view. Yes, she was definitely thinner and tired. Maybe she was coming down with something. Monsieur should see that and send her home.

51

As the music started, the couples were directed into a movement in which the woman offers only her hand, but the man is able to take the hand and reel her in like a fish (or so David thought) until she was attached at the hip. From there he could put her through a variety of moves and lifts, as demonstrated by Rennie and Gelsy. Rennie was enjoying this 'way too much, David thought. Haughtily instructing each man on how to handle "his woman" while referring to Gelsy as "my woman." David felt his temper rise, and he could see Gelsy making appealing glances to Monsieur, who only shook his head and shrugged his shoulders, as if to say, "Boys will be boys."

But when they began to dance Rennie went too far. In between the actual lifts and movements, he was touching Gelsy for no reason – putting his hand on her shoulder or the back of her neck as if to rub it. Gelsy would quickly move away but he would only step up for the next lift and do it all over again, except that each time he became a little bolder, a little more desperate.

Finally, in a running lift and slide Rennie had Gelsy where he wanted her; a faked stumble had put them up against the wall facing out the window. Rennie had Gelsy pinned to the wall under the pretext of pulling her down from a lift gone wrong but what he was actually doing, in full sight of David, was putting his hands on every intimate part of her body and, as he lowered her, forced her up against him.

In a moment David saw Rennie's hand start to disappear down inside the sash and dance trunks, then he heard Gelsy scream. By that time the entire classroom had come together to pull Rennie off the shaking girl, who ran sobbing onto Monsieur's shoulder. The horrified ballet instructor was ordering Rennie out of his class forever, but David, still in the tree, simply sat back and said coldly, "I'll kill him.

52

-17-

David sat alone at the base of the bridge, waiting for Rennie and thinking bitterly of how he would soon leave this campus in a blaze of glory. "I'll lose the only chance to make anything of myself, I'll cut down some horny, fool kid, and they'll find me in my dorm room, teaching assistant to the leading biochem instructor, higher than a kite on heroin. Yep, that ought to about do it. Should get at least twenty or thirty years for that. Maybe Adele can bake a cake with a saw in it."

He hadn't seen Rennie yet, but he would have to come this way sooner or later, since he lived at the dorm, too. David supposed Monsieur was being forced to listen to all of Rennie's sad excuses and promises to reform. Yeah, right! There, a door clanged from the dance building and footsteps... but it was Gelsy! The look of relief when she saw who was on the bridge was heartbreaking. "Davey!" she cried out, and ran to him.

David stood frozen, with a dozen fears at once. Drug enforcement agents... suppose he was being followed and they stepped up to arrest him right now? Rennie... he was waiting to shoot Rennie to defend her honor. But how could he do that in front of her?

The sight of Gelsy, her hair flying in the autumn wind, turned his knees to jelly and set his brain on fire... he definitely should not talk to her. Not now, not ever again! Robert would just have to understand. He couldn't hold his life together like this any longer. It was starting to feel like another tour of duty.

"Please, Davey, please walk me to my car. I had to park up in the north lot this morning, and now I'm afraid Rennie will be waiting to try and talk to me before I can drive away.

I can't handle that right now, something bad happened between us. I'm begging you, please, just walk me to my car."

What could he say? "I'm waiting to shoot your dance partner" didn't seem right, and no gentleman would use "I'm afraid a DEA agent might pick us both up" as an excuse. David stood speechless, and finally just looked down at his backpack to mumble, "OK."

Gelsy followed his look and quickly said, "Oh, we can go to Melville first and leave off your books," and started down the pathway. David fell in behind her. Without another word they both walked into the dorm. Luckily, Gordie was on duty and Gelsy went running to throw herself sobbing into his lap. Over his "My god, Gelsy, what…" David breezed into the elevator with, "Gotta get rid of my books, Gordie."

Once in his room he threw his backpack on his bed and ran for the bathroom. Taking the envelope out of his jacket, he tossed it in the toilet, pissed on it for good measure, and flushed it away. Only then could he feel the slightest bit safe. Hanging over his sink he felt a wave of nausea, so he threw cold water on his face, dried it, ran his fingers through his hair and sped down the stairs, forgetting completely about the gun still in his waistband.

Gelsy had her head in Gordie's lap and he was soothing her like he would a child. He looked up at David, "Do you know what he *did* to her?!" he spit out. Something in David's eyes, something very hard and cold, made him look back at Gelsy. "It's OK, *chica*. David's going to take you to your car now."

David shouldered her dance bag and the two of them walked back down the pathway, past the bus stops toward the far north parking lot. Gelsy broke the silence, "You and Gordie must think I'm being such a baby. I mean, it's not like I've been raped or anything, despite the stupid rumors Rennie was trying to pass off about New York. Nobody believed him, it was just maddening that I had to take it every day and still dance Juliet to his Romeo."

"I understand that now. I'm sorry I brushed you off yesterday. I had a hell of a headache and I'm afraid I took it out on you, Gelsy. I had no idea what you were dealing with. The guy's an ass."

"Well, we can agree on that, but at least he's no longer my Romeo. Monsieur has thrown him out of the department for good. That's why I'm afraid he'll try to find me, to get me to talk to Monsieur."

The words were barely out of her mouth when they saw a figure just ahead, lurking near a tree.

A tall, handsome profile cut against the background of foliage. Whoever it was couldn't keep still; the figure paced the walkway like a brooding ghost, one hand constantly running through a mane of black, curly hair.

Watching him turn toward them, they could see it was Rennie, and he stepped out in the middle of the walkway to wait for them.

"Gelsy, I want to speak to you. You have to talk to me. *Mi amor*, we've been through so much together!"

"No more, Rennie. *Mi amor*, no more – understand? We were never in love, we were dance partners. But you couldn't accept those terms no matter how often or in what form I gave them to you. It's been at least three years we've been having the same conversation, since we were fifteen years old, Rennie! You will not change and I am not going to live with it any longer. Go back to New York, you were happier there. And good luck."

As she tried to pass he reached out to grab her arm. David was next to him in a second, "Don't put a hand on her." His voice was cold and low, right in Rennie's ear.

"Keep out of this, old man, it's none of your business. I don't want any trouble." Rennie was proud and practically sneering at David. But although he was tall, he still had to look up to meet the older man's eyes.

"Watch out, Davey," Gelsy warned, "He carries a knife."

"I don't give a damn," David said, turning back to Rennie. "Touch her again and I'll take you down."

"Oh, by all means," Rennie answered. "And do you think I'll let you stop me from touching *my woman*?!" and here he slipped his arm neatly around Gelsy, pulling her up against his side.

What happened next Gelsy had a hard time remembering. She knew she was released from Rennie's grasp, pushed to one side and he was pulled down onto the walkway. She remembered him trying to hit David and not being able to. She remembered him trying to just get away from David and not being able to. In the scuffle Rennie had ahold of David's windbreaker and pulled it up far enough that they both saw something in the back of David's waistband. Then she remembered Rennie yelling, "Good Lord, Gelsy, he's got a *gun*!"

To this she somehow managed to answer calmly, "And your point *is*?"

Then Rennie was spread-eagled on the ground.

David was holding his neck, explaining in great detail the different ways a dancing career could end right there, with his personal favorite being the kneecaps. It took a full fifteen seconds for Rennie to admit the error of his ways and promise to never see or contact Gelsy again... ever.

When he was finally standing and brushing the dirt from his chinos, Rennie did the rare act of paying his attacker a compliment. "You're quite skilled in the martial arts, I see, David."

"I used to teach self-defense classes in the army," David answered stonily.

"I chose a bad opponent. But I will keep my promises, and I think perhaps you're right about New York, Gelsy. I was happier there. I am not the academic student you are, and I don't need Gordie to tell me I'm not cut out for a university campus."

He looked at her wistfully. "You and I both know I came here only to be with you. It has always been that way, Gelsy. Since I was a boy, I would go anywhere to be with you. After my mother died I wanted nothing more than to be with you and your family, but instead you put me with Gordie and his family. That made neither of us boys very happy. But I don't ever want to forget all your family has done for me and my sisters. Tell your mom and dad we will always have them in our prayers. And you, my dearest... partner. You're right, Gelsy, you never gave me any hope of being any more than that to me. I just couldn't stop thinking as we danced together that... whatever magic we had between us had to be real."

He looked at David with a steady gaze. "Now I see you are a different woman outside the dance studio, and you choose a different kind of man to be with. I wish you both happiness."

He turned and was gone.

Gelsy watched him for so long David started wondering if it was with regret. It was. When she turned to continue she sighed, then looked at him and said out loud, "Oh dang, why did he have to partner so well?

-18-

The day had been overcast and as they reached the parking lot the clouds looked like rain.

A chilly wind began to pick up, blowing leaves around their feet. David shivered in his light windbreaker. To distract himself he tried to decide which car was hers. The flashy Mercedes? Nah, not her style. The little Porsche? Probably neither Adele or Donald would want her in something that speedy. But he couldn't see her in a granny car either. What fit her?

A Volkswagen Jetta. "Why a Jetta?" David looked confused.

"It's cute, and it has a big back seat. When I drive to dance classes, I can curl up and take a nap in between. Getting out of the studio and having some time to relax is so important. Sometimes I'm there all day. See, I even keep a blanket back there."

She opened the back door and threw in her dance bag. He leaned against the car to admire the interior. "It is a nice little car," he said.

As he straightened up he became uncomfortably aware she had stepped in next to him, nearly pinning him to the car. The nearness of her took his breath away. It was surprisingly almost painful.

"Davey, I can't thank you enough for today. It's eliminated a cloud that's been hanging over my head for so long and the thought that I'll never have to deal with Rennie again makes me feel so free! You were pretty dang wonderful out there, too, you know."

She smiled up at him and his whole body ached. He couldn't say one word. He just watched as she put her hands on his arms, lifted herself on the balls of her feet, and kissed him.

Kissed him on the cheek, but held the position, with her hair against his lips. It was the hair, and the feeling of her body against him… he lifted his hands to her face and guided her lips to his.

Gelsy had never been kissed like that before, lips that gently took possession of hers and opened them up, searching her mouth as if reading her soul. They seemed to melt together, the wind played music around them as he ran one arm down her back. Was it the wind or did he groan? When their lips finally came apart he slid his other arm around her shoulders and pulled her even closer, burying his face in her hair. "Oh Gelsy, he whispered, "I'm sorry. That was wrong on so many levels."

The raindrops started coming down then, more of a fine mist at first that soon became drops. Above their heads they heard a shriek from a girl caught without an umbrella on the walkway. Gelsy looked up. "Cynthia! Oh, no! She's in your class, Davey, she can't see us together here. Get in the car!"

Pushing him back, Gelsy convinced the stupefied young scientist to slide into the back seat, and in a second she was seated next to him. With the doors locked and tinted windows up, she settled back with a sigh of relief. "There! Everything is OK now."

"OK," he repeated dully, shaking his head, "How can you say that? Everything is far from OK. I've blown it all. Look where I am; with the god-daughter of my professor, hiding in the back seat of her car in a parking lot."

"Davey, we kissed. Is that so bad?" She looked at him, smiling. "Was it so bad?"

"I didn't get rid of Rennie for you just so I could take his place, Gelsy."

"Of course you didn't. You kiss much better than Rennie." She giggled, then quickly turned serious. "And there's another big difference – I didn't love Rennie. I… I've fallen in love with you, Davey."

He spun around. Now his back was against the opposite door and he looked stricken.

"Don't say that, Gelsy! Don't even think that! Can't you see, if I thought that was true I'd have to go straight up to Melville, pack my stuff and catch the next bus out of here? And I've got no place else to *go*, girl!"

Gelsy had bolted forward as he was saying this, grabbing his hands in hers as if to stop him from opening the door and silencing him. "Hush, stop talking like that! How can you talk about leaving when you're the reason I'm here? *You're* what brought me home!"

"What are you talking about?"

"I was in New York, and suddenly I felt I had to go home. That was right about the time I got a letter from Buba where he said he was getting a new TA, but I paid no attention. I didn't know if it was a boy or a girl; I have no interest in his assistants. But soon after that I began feeling a strong desire to go home, that there was something there *for* me. I thought I knew everything that was here, so I couldn't imagine what it was. But I was wrong, something new had come in that time, and it was you. *You* were what called me home."

"Gelsy, you didn't know I was here. And you don't know me. You don't know anything about me. If you did, there's no way you could *love* me."

Desperate, she pulled his hands into her chest. "What is it you are so afraid of, Davey? Your past following you around? The needle marks on your arms? You don't want us to see those? Is that why you always wear a long-sleeved tee-shirt to the hoot, no matter how warm it is? And the fact you used *heroin*, you don't want us to know? How about the drug bust in the army, where you had to rat-fink on everybody else in the network in order to save your honorable discharge so you could go to college? You still feeling guilty about that?"

David was speechless; he couldn't look her in the face.

"Oh, Davey, are you such a fool that you didn't think Buba would have to do a complete background check on you before he allowed you into his precious lab? And that he wouldn't tell us before bringing you into our home?"

David raised his eyes. "And you didn't mind having a drug addict at your table?"

"Buba and Papa did dumb stuff with drugs when they were young, Davey. They even talked Mama into smuggling drugs through the Paris Airport in her bra! She got busted, and she cried and swore two American college boys got her drunk and took advantage of her. She had no idea the drugs were there! The gendarmes were so gallant they dried her tears and sent her on her way without checking her girdle. Papa and Buba still laugh about how that time they got the girl AND the girdle!"

It was funny, but David couldn't laugh. He just hung his head again, with, "And what about turning evidence on my fellow soldiers? How do I live with the fact that they went to jail with dishonorable discharges and I went free and went to college on the GI Bill?"

"I have no problem with that. They would never have made of themselves what you have made of yourself. I even looked them up. All three of them had been in and out of jail before they met you and have been since."

David shook his head. "I can't believe you and your family have known this the whole time."

"Yes." She lifted his hands and kissed them. "But we all loved the man we met and got to know. Especially me."

He sat there for the longest time, trying to process this. Thinking about the times he'd sat in the dorm lobby, listening to guys wonder what it would take to just get a date with this beautiful girl. And now he'd kissed her, was sitting in the back seat of a car with her, holding her hands, listening to her say she was falling for him – *him*!… and then a sickening thought struck.

He kept his eyes down. "You're not just playing a game with me, are you, Gelsy?"

She dropped his hands and drew back. "Did you ever see 'West Side Story?"

He searched his brain. "What, the movie?"

"The musical, yes. Tony asks Maria just that when they meet. She says, 'I never learned to play games like that. I think now I never will."

He kept his eyes down, but bit his lips. She reached over to him and ran one finger gently over his mouth, then kissed him again, and again. "Davey, I feel now as though when they made me in heaven, they engraved your name on my heart and you are there forever. For some reason you have become precious to me. I want you to stay. Please promise me."

"Girl, don't do this. I can't promise you." His voice was getting lower, and he was afraid.

"What will it take to convince you not to run away, Davey? Because I don't want to let you leave now. I'm worried they'd go looking for you later and your room would be bare."

"Gelsy…"

"And it wouldn't do any good, Davey. Because wherever you went, I'd find you and bring you back."

"Gelsy, why?" His eyes were closed tightly now, almost like he was afraid of crying.

"I don't know why. That's just the way it is. I love you, and I think… I think I want to belong to you now so you won't leave me later."

She reached up and started to pull off her jacket, throwing it on the seat behind her. David's eyes shot open as she took the bottom of her tank-top and pulled it over her head. She wasn't wearing a bra. Then she slithered out of her track suit pants, shedding socks and canvas loafers on the way. Now she was perched on the seat naked, looking at him.

David tried to close his eyes again; tearing himself apart. She was beautiful and within reach but untouchable. She was offering herself to him but he had no right to even think about taking her, shouldn't even be looking at her like this…

"Girl…" he half-choked on the words, "*What are you thinking?*"

She spoke matter-of-factly, but was beginning to shiver, "I'm thinking that if you make love to me now you won't leave me. I'm thinking that I already feel like I belong to you and it's just a matter of time and place, anyway. If you take what belongs to you in the back seat of a car, or sometime in the future in a fancy hotel room, what's the difference?"

"What's the difference?! Gelsy, who do you think I am? I'm not *having sex* with you here. I'm not a guy who goes around with a condom in my wallet. I've only had sex with whores, in the army. And they're always prepared for that. I've got no way to protect you."

"Then I can go directly to Student Health for a morning-after shot and get a prescription for birth-control pills while I'm there. Anyway, according the rhythm method, I'm at the low end of my fertility cycle."

"*What?* Are you crazy, girl?"

63

Now she had to hug herself. The rain was falling fast outside and the air was chilly in the car.

"I'll understand if you don't find me very attractive right now, Davey." She hung her head and her beautiful hair hid her face. "I've lost a lot of weight, worrying about Rennie and I'll never be well-endowed, anyway. The French say a woman's breast should just fit a champagne glass, you know." She wiped away a tear. "But if you're used to professionals, I can understand…"

"You think I don't *want* you?! My God…" He couldn't stand any more. His arms gathered her in and he warmed her skin with his hands. Reaching to the floor, he pulled the blanket around her. "Feel me, Gelsy. Feel me and tell me if I want you or not." He shifted her body up against him so she could feel his erection, and she nestled against his chest there, soaking up all his warmth. "Good God, girl…"

For a moment all she could do was feel the amazing sensation of being pressed against him, smelling him, running her hands over his torso. Then she was unbuttoning his shirt, putting her cheek against his chest and kissing his bare skin. "Oh Davey, it is so nice to touch you." And again she kissed his chest and neck, this time more wildly.

At first he pulled her in and pressed her closer with both hands, then just as suddenly he pushed her away. Confused, she knelt on the seat and pushed the hair out of her eyes to see he was ripping his own clothes off; first his shirt, then laying his gun on the floor of the car, unzipping his pants, and, looking her square in the face, sliding out of his pants and jockey shorts at once.

Gelsy had seen naked men before. Around theatres and dance studios quite often dressing room doors will open at inappropriate times. She had even seen some naked men that could be called "studly," but David put them to shame. She froze in rapt concentration of his male beauty.

David, flushing and misunderstanding, whispered, "Afraid now, girl?"

"No, *mon Cherie*, It is just that you are so… lovely. Like a living statue." Her eyes filled with tears.

David pulled her close, kissed her, pressed her against him and then gently pushed her backwards onto the seat and sliding down next to her.

Suddenly he realized that all his experience had been with women much more experienced than he was in the art of making love. They initiated foreplay, asked him what he wanted, and went out of their way to make him comfortable. He had never before been the one in charge. Holding this beautiful creature in his arms, he had never wanted anything more than to love her but hesitated in his taking of her.

For several minutes he simply lay next to her on the blanket and fondled her, kissing her breasts and shoulders, his hands working their way over every inch of her skin. Fear of discovery was never far from his mind... Suppose campus police knocked on the windows and ordered them to open the doors? But having her naked beside him like this was worth any price.

Finally, unable to wait any long and preparing to mount her, he forced himself to stop long enough to whisper, "I… don't want to hurt you…"

She reached up to touch his shoulders and whispered back, "Just hurt me in the nicest possible way."

-19-

Afterward, he gathered up his clothes from the floor of the car and saw her take a towel from the dance bag. She carefully wiped herself and, folding it, handed it to him. He couldn't look at her as he wiped himself and dropped it on the car floor. There it unfolded and he saw the tiny streaks of blood mixed with the pearly white liquid.

The towel. Would she notice if he kept the towel?

She probably would, but he'd cop to it later. He couldn't stand the thought of it being washed.

All the evidence of their first encounter, of her giving herself to him, he had to keep it. Otherwise, how would he know it really happened? When he was alone in his dorm, would he trust his memory with something as precious as this? Luckily it was a hand towel and easily wrapped around his gun. She wouldn't see it when it was tucked into the back of his waistband.

"Davey?" He whirled around. Had she seen him? No, she was looking out the window at the rain and seemed deep in thought.

"What is it, Gelsy?

"What that the first time you've ever been with a woman, without… you know… using protection?"

"What? You mean without a condom?! Yes, of course! I told you, I've only had sex with hookers and I was always careful not to catch anything. You don't have to worry about that, girl."

No, that's not it." She turned to face him, not even trying to cover her nakedness. I was thinking, it's like I took your virginity, too."

"You… what are you talking about?"

66

"Well, this is the first time you actually joined with someone, that your skin was touching someone else's skin and that when it was over, you left part of yourself inside that person. Isn't that right?"

He thought about it. It was not only true, but heartbreakingly real. He reached out for her and pulled her back in to his chest. "Yes it's true. I just never thought about it like that, Gelsy."

She snuggled into his bare chest, their two naked bodies wrapping around each other like plants intertwining. Thinking about how he'd just made love to her could only arouse him again. She responded by kissing him softly, then stroking him and kneeling so she could press down against him. Sitting like this, she had all the control. David simply allowed her to experiment while he sat back and stroked her breasts in quiet joy. So unbelievably lovely…

When it was all over he re-dressed awkwardly in the backseat, struggling with underwear, jeans, shirt, windbreaker, socks, shoes and – of course – the gun. She, by comparison, slid into her tank top and track suit as if it were a second skin, and he wondered at how cool she could be to undress and dress again in front of him. Then he remembered the evening they'd raced in the pool and she stripped her wet tee-shirt off, leaving just a transparent camisole covering her chilled breasts before her mother could throw a towel over her.

To her mom's protestations of indecency, she laughingly reminded everyone there of how often dancers were forced to make quick costume changes in the wings of the stage, with other performers and crew standing just inches away. "We have our noses in each other's armpits," she sniffed, holding her own delicate nostrils on high, "And just about everywhere *else*, too!" David had been speechless with laughter for at least a full minute.

"Davey?" Her voice brought him back to the present.

"What, Gelsy?"

"Do you intend to make an honest woman of me?"

David felt like he'd been hit by a baseball bat. "Make an honest… you mean, *marry* you?"

"That is exactly what I mean." She suddenly looked serious, and even a little frightened.

Without thinking, he swept the girl into his arms and held her so tight she couldn't breathe. "My God, Gelsy, don't you know I'd marry you today even if it meant giving up my scholarship and pumping gas for the rest of my life?"

She firmly pushed herself apart far enough to look him in the eyes in total bewilderment. "Why would you do such a terrible thing… give up your scholarship?" she asked.

He brushed the hair back from her face and had to laugh, "My darling girl, even though you eat very little, I still can't afford to feed you on what I make as a TA. Hell, I can barely feed myself! And you couldn't live with me at the dorm, so it would mean getting an apartment. I'm afraid I don't have enough in my bank account to cover everything."

"And you wouldn't have to. I have my own trust fund, thank you very much. Plus I have an inheritance left to me by my grandmother. Plus I am the sole heir of both my parent's and Buba's estates. I could probably support half the UCSM student body if I had to."

David was taken aback by this new thought. "Don't tell me I'm marrying for money."

"No, my darling, because when you get your degree you'll have no trouble getting a good position and your own money. Buba has absolute faith in your abilities and he ought to know. I just wanted to think that you had honorable intentions."

He looked at her with so much love there wasn't really any need for words, but the few he had were just what she wanted to hear. "I love you, and I've never said that to another living soul. You've got to know I want to marry you, Gelsy… I want you more than I've ever wanted anything in my whole life." They sealed the bargain with a very long kiss.

Now she was ready and so was he. She took one last, long look into his eyes, kissed him again and oozed into the driver's seat like a cat. He silently opened the back door and stepped out into the damp, grey parking lot.

It wasn't until he heard the door close behind him that he felt it… the cold, sudden pain deep in his chest. He grabbed his left elbow with his right hand and pulled his arm around his stomach, thinking he must look like a man on the verge of a heart attack. Walking behind the car, he recoiled with the same panic he felt during his PTSD episodes as the engine started. He wasn't in Afghanistan, he was in a parking lot at a university. But the space between him and the pathway leading back to the dorm stretched on forever and she was putting the car into drive.

"Gelsy!" He had whirled around and taken two stumbling steps back toward the car. That was enough, the car stopped on the wet pavement, the engine idled and the window rolled down.

"Gelsy…" He held his hands on the window frame, as if to keep the window from rolling up again. He had to tell her how hurt he felt because she wasn't in his arms any longer. That his body had developed a need for her worse than heroin, and how he'd never felt so alone. This was impossible. He'd survived three tours of duty in combat. Now he wondered if he could make it back to the dorm without the ground opening up and swallowing him.

He bowed his head and was suddenly humbled by tears, but her forehead was pressing against his and he could feel her pull at something around her neck. In a moment she'd taken off her crucifix, turned it around and put it over his head. Pressing the gold cross to her lips she whispered, "God, this is now the dearest person in my life. I beg you to watch over him every moment of every day. Keep him safe for me, because I can't live without him. I ask this in the name of Our Lord Jesus. Amen." Tucking the chain inside his shirt, she smiled at him through her own tears, said, I'll see you in three and half hours," rolled up her window and drove through the exit leading to the Student Health Center.

Turning back to the walkway, he was amazed to see that the distance had shrunk to only maybe thirty feet from where he was standing.

-20-

Gordie had been waiting for him. He should have remembered both Gordie and Mark would want a blow-by-blow description of his encounter with Rennie. Was that only an hour and a half ago? No, it was in another life, but how could he make them understand?

"Hey, guys," he poked his head in Gordie's dorm room and the television was immediately switched to *mute*. "Any chance I could buy some quarters so I could run a load of laundry before I have to leave for dinner?"

"Not until we get the full and complete story," Mark said, standing and ready to present him with a can of discount-store beer. "Query first, quarters later."

"Quarters first because I'll run out of time, but I'll tell you that it all went well, and Rennie's probably packing his bags right now."

"Praise be! Gordie, get this man his quarters. David, you have ten minutes to come back with the complete, unvarnished story."

Ten minutes. I'll have to try and get back to planet Earth in just ten minutes, he thought on his way to his room.

David focused his mind and changed into a track suit, putting the towel into his shaving kit and everything he'd been wearing into a basket along with his other laundry to take down to the washing machine.

"Five minutes." He tried to make sure he was using laundry detergent instead of dish soap, as he'd done once in his younger days. His mind was so muddled he didn't trust himself on even the smallest detail right now.

"One minute." He only had to walk back up the stairs. Now he had to walk back in the door, where they quickly shut the TV completely off and prepared themselves for a recitation. He accepted the luke-warm beer, sipped it thoughtfully and cleared his throat while they fidgeted.

"We'd nearly made it to the parking lot, and Rennie came out from behind a tree. Said he wanted to talk to Gelsy and told me to get lost. I took him down to the ground and said if he ever bothered her again I'd grind his kneecaps into the concrete. Told him he'd have a hard time making it as a dancer after that. He got up, apologized and ran. Case closed."

Gordie and Mark had been lapping up every word like kittens lapping up cream. When he got to the "Kneecaps into concrete" part, they were in each other's laps, choking with pure happiness and cheap beer.

"Do you really think he's packing, Gordie?" Mark asked hopefully.

"How can he not? Without dance classes, he's got no credits to speak of. No academic ones, that's for sure."

"And you're through helping him, right?" David asked archly.

"Fellow Latino love goes only so far, and I never wanted him as a brother-in-law, anyway. Luisa will just have to get over him. He never gave a damn for her anyway. It was always *Gelsy, Gelsy, Gelsy.*"

David winced at hearing that name spoken out loud. Pretending it was the flat, crummy beer causing him intense heartburn, he stood up and grimaced. "I'm going back to my room for a shower and change of clothes… and a decent beer," calling over his shoulder as he made a hasty exit.

It was good to be alone in his room. He took the towel out of the shaving kit. Sitting on the edge of his bed, he held it as if it were a religious icon. The thought made him take the crucifix out of his shirt and study it, too. He had two things to hold onto, to hold back the pain of not having her beside him. *Why couldn't I have had something to give her?* he thought with a quick stab of pain. She had driven off with nothing, he had even stolen her towel! Pounding his forehead with his hand he said, *Idiot! Are you that dumb, you couldn't even give her your old army lighter?*

His cell phone rang. Was Robert cancelling dinner plans… had he found out?!

No, it was Gelsy. He didn't even think she knew his cell number. Why would she be calling so fast? Had she already realized what a terrible mistake she'd made? Was she breaking it off already? "Hi, girl," he mumbled into the phone, head bowed and prepared for the worse.

"Darling," the soft sound of her voice soothed him, "I was afraid you'd start thinking that I gave you a cross that was precious to me and you'd given me nothing, but you're wrong."

How had she known? She was amazing.

"I'm leaving the Student Health Center. I got the morning-after shot and a prescription for pills, but that doesn't change the fact that you have left me with something.

"You've given me part of your body, your DNA. What could be more precious? Especially to know that it was the first time you'd ever shared yourself like that. I feel so happy because you've made me *yours*, actually part of you. Can you understand that, darling?"

He tried to catch his breath. "No, girl, not really. I can't understand why you'd want to be… *mine*. But if it makes you happy, you can't imagine how it makes me feel." His voice was breaking up. "Three hours, Gelsy," and clicked off.

Then he broke down and cried.

Gordie came in while he was in the shower, yelling over the noise, "OK if I come in for a second?"

"Sounds like you're already in." David shut off the shower, wrapped a towel around his waist and walked into the room to grab his clothes.

"David!" Gordie stood up like a man who'd taken a shot from behind, realizing he was dying.

"What?!?" asked David, truly frightened by the ashen tone that had stolen over his friend's face.

Gordie looked at his neck. "That's Gelsy's crucifix!"

David stood there, holding the towel and not knowing whether to be proud or ashamed.

"She gave it to me," he said, as casually as possible. Walking back into the bathroom, he dressed with unusual speed and came out with his white shirt buttoned up over the cross.

It didn't work. Gordie immediately reached into the shirt and pulled out the relic.

"Do you know how much this cost Gelsy's dad, David? Over twenty grand. Do you really want to walk around with that much hanging from your neck? Even Gelsy sometimes has anxiety attacks about wearing it."

"What am I going to do, Gordie? She put it around my neck and blessed it."

As soon as he said the last part, he knew it was pretty much all over. They both sat down on the edge of the bed.

"What happened out there, really, David?" A long silence followed.

"Is it Ok if we don't talk about it right now, Gordie?"

"You know how I feel about her, David. If I ever thought you did anything…"

"I love her, a hundred times more than you and Mark put together. She says she loves me. I want to marry her." He sat up straight. "I'm going to marry her, Gordie. There, that's it."

Once more Gordie's face took on the look of a man stricken, but this time expecting the blow. He rocked back and forth on the soles of his feet, clasping and unclasping his hands.

"Mark was right. Everything comes so easy for you. Everything he and I wanted for so long."

He stood up and walked out.

-21-

When Robert's car got them to the house, dinner was actually ready and on the sideboard for once. Gelsy had claimed overwhelming hunger pains and had started eliminating the appetizers before Robert could even grab a plate. Without anyone noticing she'd grabbed David's arm in the hallway, though, bouncing up and down like a puppy. Any sad thoughts quickly left his mind in the joy of her presence. He relaxed and smiled at her with no trace of strain or bitterness. She was so unbelievably lovely.

While they were eating she entertained them with a rather embellished version of David's encounter with Rennie. "Just exactly like a knight in shining armor," she held forth, waving half a grilled-cheese sandwich. "Of course it means I won't be dancing the balcony scene…. no, there's absolutely *nobody* else who can handle the MacMillan choreography… but it's the price I'm willing to pay to never put up with him again. Yes, he'll lose his scholarship and I'm sorry for that, but he never could have graduated with his terrible academic record. He relied on other people to do *all* his work for him…. mostly girls in love with him…. mostly Luisa! Poor girl"

And here she could resist the grilled-cheese no longer so Robert was able to ask, "But truly, Gelsy, you had your heart set on finally getting to dance Juliet, so don't tell me you're not disappointed tonight."

"Buba, I am happy tonight!" (And here she gave David a gentle nudge under the table.) Do you not see me eating everything in sight? I don't have to worry about fitting into a Juliet costume! And I'm only eighteen, I'll have another chance."

As if in fateful answer to her words, the telephone rang. Her mother looked at her sternly.

"*Mon Cherie*, I thought I asked you to turn that thing off!"

"Mama, I had to leave it on for Monsieur. He was very upset about Rennie and wanted to call and check on me."

She was up in a flash and David could hear her running through a conversation in French at super-sonic speed that sounded like anything but a comforting message.

Flushed, she ran back to the table and threw herself into her seat.

"You will *never* guess what happened," she said.

"Well, we won't if you don't tell us," Robert replied, laying down his fork and looking concerned.

"I *will* be dancing Juliet after all."

"And your Romeo will be…"

She waited so long and turned so pink David began to worry Monsieur had convinced her to forgive Rennie, but she finally lowered her head and whispered, "Naj."

"Naj?! What is he doing in Los Angeles?!?"

"The Hollywood people have been trying forever to sign him to a movie contract. Now he's agreed to meet with them and tomorrow he takes class with Madame. Afterward, he'll stay for lunch, then he and I will rehearse. He already knows the choreography, of course."

"Of course. Learned it from MacMillan himself, right?" Robert's expression was impossible to read. Was he being sarcastic? David had the feeling there was no love lost between "Buba" and the Russian.

"Actually, yes. Naj was probably the last person to learn it directly from MacMillan. But so did Monsieur and Madame, for that matter. They both danced with the Royal Ballet during his time. I'm very lucky to have a chance to learn from three descendants."

"I know, and I'm sorry, sweetie. You take all of that very seriously and I shouldn't make fun of it. It just seems like a little too much to throw at you, going from Rennie to the world's greatest male ballet dancer. And the performance is only – what? Only three weeks away?

"From tomorrow. And a one-shot event. But no pressure." And here she looked regretfully at her plate. "And no more grilled-cheese, either."

-22-

Later, as they were getting settled on the patio David had a chance to whisper to her, "What's this going to really mean… for us?"

"Only that I'll be rehearsing extra on Saturday afternoons for three weeks. But you usually spend Saturdays doing work for Buba, don't you? Maybe you could take the bus downtown afterward and come home with me…" here she grinned at him, "in my car?"

David was relieved. She'd already thought of time for them to be together.

And then she began to sing. Strumming the guitar softly, she sang a Civil War ballad of a young girl in love with a soldier -- so in love she vows to follow him into battle. She'll disguise herself in a uniform, pull back her hair in a cap and fight next to him, but all he will answer is, "No, my love, no." Finally she breaks down and accuses the young man not of love but of selfishness, of not caring enough about what *she* wants. Suddenly his answer is "Yes, my love, yes." And together, side by side, they march off to the cruel war.

David was, as always, drawn in by her beautiful voice. But this time he couldn't look away from those hypnotic, multicolored eyes. It was so obvious she sang to him from her heart, that she was telling him he wasn't to leave without taking her, wherever he went. As she sang the last notes he thought perhaps soon he could finally say to himself, "She loves me."

In the silence that followed Donald cleared his throat and spoke up, "David, Gelsy wanted to sing that tonight because of what we were watching on the news yesterday. It seems the military is calling up veterans for extra tours of duty because they can't get new recruits into the field fast enough and we wondered, is there a possibility that you might be… ??"

In a rush, it was all true. David looked around at each in amazement. Gelsy loved him… they all really cared about him. He couldn't find any words at first and played with his wineglass. But Gelsy flushed and sat up, nearly dropping her guitar on the tiles, "Why don't you say something, Davey??"

David took a long sip of wine and tried to clear his throat. Robert had already begun to speak, "True, I did hear from a friend in Washington something was happening, and that a few re-ups had already been mailed." He looked thoughtfully at David. "Some were even due this weekend."

The guitar hit the tiles with a sickening *crunck*. Gelsy was standing now, her eyes filling rapidly.

"Is that it, Davey? When you got back to your dorm this afternoon, was there something in the mail you didn't want to talk about?" The look on her face suddenly reminded David of Gordie's look when he saw the crucifix. He immediately stood to face her with his arms out.

"Gelsy, I'm 4-F! Three tours, wounded and PTSD. I'm sorry I didn't say anything, but you took me by surprise."

If he had anything more to say he couldn't have gotten it out, because she had thrown herself into his arms with so much force he barely stayed upright. Her father gave a nervous little chuckle at her sudden rush into the embrace of their guest and said, "Honey, you've got too much hair to hide in a cap, anyway."

"Then I'd cut it all off, or shave my head if I had to, Papa!" she sobbed back at him.

Holding her as close as possible and kissing the very top of her head, David muttered, "Crazy girl! Like I'd *ever* let her within a *thousand miles* of Afghanistan!!"

"If you were there, they couldn't keep me out, Davey."

He shook his head in amazement, sat back on the sofa and pulled her down into his lap, where she quickly curled up as if she'd sat there all her life.

Her startled father looked at her mother, who looked at Robert, who looked back at Donald, who finally said, "Is there… something… we should… *know*??"

Gelsy peeked out from under David's chin to say firmly, "I love him, Papa. Only him, and I always will. I belong to him and I always will. Everybody, that's what you need to know."

David gave a deep sigh that sounded like a half-strangled groan. "That's not exactly what they wanted to hear, girl." Shifting her weight to the sofa cushions he stood up to face the others.

"You all know exactly who I am," he said, his hands in his pockets and his eyes not quite able to meet theirs. "You know about how I tried to make something of my life in the army and how I came close to losing everything there. You know I haven't got anything right now to offer Gelsy, not even a decent name. 'Collins' was the name of a foster family who took me in when I was thirteen, but I ran away from them as soon as I could. I lived on the streets until I was eighteen and joined the army. That led me to college and here."

Everyone was paying respectful attention. He could feel their interest, now that he was finally opening up to them. Forcing himself to bring his eyes up to their level he continued, "If you think I've worked hard before now to get where I am, I promise I'll work ten times harder if I know I'll have Gelsy to provide for. You heard her say she loves me, but there's no words to tell you how much I love her; and need her, now, in my life. I'd like your permission to marry her."

He sat down and Gelsy promptly crawled back on his lap. Mother, father and godfather regarded them with the kind of awe usually seen in devotees of fine art objects, and indeed they made a lovely sight.

Donald finally broke the spell by saying, "Well, I think it's a done deal and we'd better break out the champagne!" as Adele broke into a combination of tears and giggles. Only Robert remained completely silent, except for an absent-minded soft strumming on his guitar. "What's the matter, Robert? Cat got your tongue?"

"No, Donald. I was just wondering when somebody was going to ask me what I thought of all this."

A sad and worried look crossed David's face. "Robert, you know how important your opinion is to everybody here, especially to me. Would I be here if it weren't for you? Gelsy even thinks God made you his instrument in bringing us together."

Robert's face beamed and he struck a loud chord. "That's my god-daughter!" Another higher chord. "She knows the hand of God when she sees it!" Winking at Donald and Adele, he sat the guitar down and prepared to pontificate. "I have a condition. No, wait, I have *two* conditions." He held up a finger. "The first one is that you complete your doctoral program as planned." He pointed the finger at David.

"Of course, Robert! That goes without saying. How else could I provide for Gelsy unless I get my degree?"

"Well, you could run off and get married now and join some professional military unit as a trainer for one thing, but that would be bad. I want you to wait just a little while because… well, because I want you to graduate as Dr. David *Chaveral.*"

An immediate chorus of "What?" and "Who?" rocketed across the patio, but Robert waved them all away and countered, "You just heard David say he didn't have a decent name to offer Gelsy. Well, I want him to take mine. I want to adopt him. He'll be my son, and when he marries Gelsy she'll be *Gelsy Chaveral*, my daughter-in-law." He presented this new thought to them with a flourish of his hands, and if he'd ignited a bombshell it couldn't have landed with more force.

"Robert, you old son-of-a-bitch… you've *done it*! You've united our two families at last!!" Throwing down his guitar Donald went for his friend's torso with a huge bear hug that lifted Robert off the tiles. Adele could only weep with undisguised joy, but now Gelsy had her arms around her mother's neck and was weeping along with her. Only David stood alone, dazed.

"*ADOPT* me? Are you joking? Can you even do that?" he was saying more to himself than to anyone in particular.

"Oh, yes, it's quite legal and quite doable, David. As a matter of fact, I've already seen my lawyers about doing it, and it won't even take that long. I don't have any other family to fight you over my estate; Gelsy is my sole heir and I don't think she's going to object to sharing her inheritance with her husband."

"Buba, Buba, say that again… that sounds so good!" Gelsy was choking out the words between tears.

"Which, my sweet? 'Inheritance' or 'husband'?" Robert came up behind both women and began kissing them into fits of laughter. Gelsy ran to David and wrapped her arms around his waist.

"Don't you see, my love? You're bringing us all together in reality, as a family…. just like we always wanted!" David's eyes opened wide, but not with the joy Gelsy expected.

There was nothing David could say. They were giving him the family he never had, the woman he adored. Robert had already given him a job, a doctoral program and the opportunity of a career, and now he was offering to give him his name? Gelsy had told the people most important in her life that she loved him. It was more than he could accept. The old panic set in.

"I think I need to talk to my counselor." The words were out of his mouth; he heard them when everybody else did. Silence. Standing stricken in the center of the patio, he'd unwrapped Gelsy's arms and was holding her slightly apart from him. His eyes were darting from one face to the other, pleading with them to understand the fear. Robert, bless him, understood immediately.

"It's all too much, isn't it, son?" he said, using the word *son* for the first time, but making it sound so natural no one found it out of place. "You're being hit on all sides by changes, and that's hard to handle. Even good changes can be scary. It doesn't feel natural, does it? You don't have much experience in being... happy."

Now the others relaxed, because they saw David take this in and accept the rationale. He sank back down on the sofa and pulled Gelsy down with him. She snuggled her way back up on his lap and he held her like he'd never let go.

The other three looked among themselves in an unspoken form of communication. Meeting as young people of a hippie "Love" generation had left them with a different history than even Gelsy knew, and a completely different set of values from most families. They all agreed.

Donald spoke up. "You know, Davey, I think you should start sharing our home part-time. Stay in Gelsy's room a few nights a week and just use your dorm room when you've got studying to do or late-night research sessions with Robert. There's no shame; Adele and I lived together for nearly two years before we were married."

David looked up with a face full of almost-pathetic relief. They knew he couldn't let go of her…

"Gelsy, get him a pair of my pajamas and a new toothbrush from the guest bathroom for tonight; Robert can take him to get some things from his dorm tomorrow." Nodding at Gelsy he said, "You guys want to turn in now? David looks beat."

Beat wasn't even close, David thought. The day seemed to have dawned a month ago. Why had he spent most of it packing a gun? Had he known when he woke up that he'd be buying heroin in the morning, beating up Rennie and then becoming Gelsy's lover by mid-day in the back of a car? A shudder disturbed Gelsy from her position on his lap, so he took the opportunity to stand up and pull her to him. "Want to take your dad's advice?" he asked, looking very tired.

Gelsy said not a word but blew kisses to the others and led him away, into the house. Stopping only to run into her parent's bedroom for a clean pair of pajamas and the guest bathroom for the required toothbrush, she guided him down the second-story hall to her room.

David was immensely relieved to see it was at the opposite end of the house from her parent's room, and really formed almost a little wing of its own facing away from the pool area. She had her own little microwave, refrigerator, table, chairs, a little sink by all these as well as one in her own bathroom. A miniature ballet studio, made from a converted storage area, had been lovingly set up in the hall between her room and the guest bathroom and bedroom. It was obvious the girl spent much of her time being self-sufficient.

"I'll go take a shower in the guest bathroom so you can have the bathroom in here tonight, darling." Gelsy had towels out and was off before he could offer a protest, not that he had any. The shower Gordie had interrupted in his dorm room had been brief and not even lukewarm. A long, hot shower sounded like a gift from heaven.

Gelsy's bathroom was spacious and surprisingly free from the toiletry collections most girls her age can't seem to live without, cluttering up every square inch of bathroom space. Soap, shampoo and conditioner were in the shower, and some lotion on the sideboard was about all. David was glad; no need to gild this lily. He showered, then remembered the pajamas. He'd left them lying on the bed. Wrapping a towel around his waist he walked to the bedroom just in time to see Gelsy, in identical attire, come dancing though the hall doorway, She outdid him by an extra towel wrapped around her long, heavy hair, which, when wet, seemed to take on Medusa-like size.

He couldn't stop himself from staring. He'd seen her strip in the back of the car, but for some odd reason she seemed more naked now, with just a towel wrapped around that tiny body. His voice got a little husky as he tried to make his feelings known to her. "You look so beautiful right now, girl, and it makes me think that there's something I've always wanted to try…"

She'd been on her way to her dresser, but paused now, uncertainly, with her leg pressed lightly against the corner of the bed. Standing like that, she pulled the towel from her head and shook her Rapunzel-like hair. It floated down her back and shoulders. David was overwhelmed with an emotion that went past love, lust or anything else he could put a name to. She was simply the most desirable creature he could have ever imagined, and she loved him. She loved *him*? How was he ever going to learn to live with that?

He didn't want to frighten her, but the feelings she was stirring were becoming evident under his only covering, so he gently stepped forward and pushed her down until she was sitting on the edge of the bed. She still looked confused, and held onto the top of the towel although the bottom had opened to expose her thighs. When she realized it was there David was kneeling to reach and open she shivered, unsure if she was ready for this. Very softly David said, "I told you, girl, I've only had sex with whores in the army before you. *This* is something I'd never want to do with a whore, but I want so much to try it with you right now. I won't do anything you don't want me to do, though…"

He was asking her permission. She'd told him she belonged to him, but Gelsy had to overcome a natural fear. This was unexpected and strange, yet she wanted to make him happy, and he said he'd do nothing if she didn't allow it!

She carefully unwrapped the towel and laid it on the floor, sitting uncertainly in the nude before him. David reached up and lovingly ran his hands down her body, from her shoulders and breasts to her thighs, which he gently opened. Kissing her inner thighs and stroking with his fingertips what was between them, he felt his own breath quicken. What he was looking at was so lovely, it made him happy he'd never paid much attention to that part of the anatomy on women he'd used in the army to relieve himself. Gelsy had the soft fur and pink lips of a woodland creature; there was nothing disgusting about kissing her there. She was beautiful… so beautiful…

He slid his hands up to her armpits and lifted her back onto the bed, spreading her out so he could explore her completely. For nearly twenty minutes he did nothing but take inventory of this woman who said she loved him, using his eyes, hands and mouth but always coming back to that lovely spot between her thighs. Finally she began to anticipate it, and whimpered like a stroked cat when he came near it.

That pleased him. He was able to give her pleasure in more than one way. He hoped he'd find many more; pleasing her was amazingly happy work.

At one point she indicated she wanted to return the favor, but his size made that difficult and he whispered to her there was time for it later. Now he was past the point of waiting any longer; he simply needed to be inside of her. It was easier now; she was so ready. Having the comfortable space of a bed and knowing what they were doing was known and sanctioned took away any of the doubts David had held earlier. This was right. This was what people meant when they talked about "making *love*."

Neither one wore the clean pajamas they'd laid out. Instead, when they'd finished with each other, they pulled the covers over their bodies and snuggled down together like two contented children. When David woke up in the morning, he found his face half-buried in her soft, fragrant hair. "What a way to start the day," he thought sleepily to himself, and would have stayed right there if she hadn't wanted to turn over to cuddle up to him. "That's pretty good, too," he thought again, stroking her bare shoulders. "If I could wake up like this every day for the rest of my life, I think I might finally know what it's like to be a happy man."

Holding her close, smelling the scent of her and feeling the aching need led to only one outcome. They joined again and he took his time and savored his ability to take her at will. She was so eager to please him, and beautiful beyond anything he could have ever dreamed. There was such a dreamlike quality to this new life.

-23-

Afterwards, they took separate showers and dressed in the bathrooms by agreement, going down for breakfast so that there would be no accidental meetings on the way. David arrived in the dining area to find Gelsy and her mom whispering and giggling over their coffee, while Donald stood at the stove with blueberry pancakes sizzling in a pan.

"Don't go over there," he warned, "Girl-talk at its worse! Your coffee is waiting for you on the breakfast bar and I've got pancakes coming right up. Robert called to say he'd be here in about fifteen or twenty minutes, so you have time to eat. Adele will drive Gelsy over to Madame's for class and rehearsal." He flipped the pancakes onto a plate and presented them to David like a short-order cook. "Your order, sir."

David accepted them gravely. "And I'll see your service is reflected in your tip, my good man." Picking up the bottle of maple syrup he baptized them soundly and murmured, "*Mmmmm!*"

The two men sat down together at the breakfast bar like old friends in a diner. "So," Donald began, "Did you sleep well in you new abode?"

"Yes, sir," David managed, through a mouthful of crisp dough. "Nice place you have here. I must come back more often." He looked at Donald and smiled happily.

Donald nodded in agreement. "Gelsy floated down the stairs this morning, singing like a lark… something about being in love with a wonderful guy, I think. Would that be you?"

"Wow, I certainly hope so." Turning serious, "God knows I love her, sir."

Before Donald could reassure him, Robert had burst on the scene. "What's this? I find you all still at breakfast at this late hour? Gelsy, your class starts in ten minutes," (sharp gasps as the women jumped up to search for purses) "And my assistant is stuffing himself with pancakes? This will not do, Donald! He'll be asleep on his feet from the carb overload. From now on, you make sure he gets only protein shakes on days we have marathon lab work ahead of us."

David was standing but surprisingly hesitated to ask. "Gelsy, is there any way you can get away to come to campus? Maybe at lunch, even for a few minutes?"

Everyone in the room stopped, confused. It was obvious Gelsy would have to spend the day at Madame's studio, downtown. To leave, go all the way to campus and go back again was a terrible imposition. Why was he even asking?

"Davey, I'll do whatever you want, but please tell me why."

Donald spoke up, "Yes, I'll go get her myself if it's important, but I want to know, too. Is it because you want to see her before she sees Naj?"

David looked startled. "No, not at all. It's just..." and he looked down, searching for words.

"You'll want me to go to Mass with you in the morning, won't you? And that's fine. I understand. But if I do, I think Gelsy should be wearing a ring." He looked up. "And I still have some money put away, from my discharge allowance…"

He didn't get any further because Gelsy was in his arms, half-choking him and sobbing. Robert stood there tapping his foot, finally saying out loud, "Boy, did *you* say something right!" Donald and Adele just beamed.

Running to the what-not drawer, Gelsy picked up a piece of notepaper, a Magic-Marker and a pair of scissors. Drawing a line on the paper, she cut it out, wrapped it around her ring finger, carefully marked where the end hit and took a piece of tape to create a little circle. Gravely she handed it to David.

"You don't need me, darling, all you need is my ring size. I want to wear the ring *you* choose for me. And it doesn't have to even be new. Look in pawn shops for something old and interesting, something with a history. I like yellow gold and I don't really like diamonds, at least not big ones. They look cold, like pieces of ice. My birthstone is garnet, but any stone would do, as long as the ring looks special to you."

David took the paper and tucked it into his shirt pocket, kissed her goodbye without a word, and turned to follow Robert to the car. Somehow everyone knew he was too choked up to say another word at that minute, so they let him go. Robert, however, after driving a few miles down the road turned to him and proudly said, "That god-daughter of mine is one in a million, isn't she?

-24-

At the studio, Naj was more than ready for her. He looked like a carnivore who had been kept on a vegetarian diet for a few months and now had a juicy steak dangled in front of him. From the sweat-soaked blonde Russian curls to his fabulously flexible feet, every exquisite muscle that had women all over the world sighing was primed and aching toward one thing... *Gelsy*. She walked through the door like a hamburger walking into a tiger's mouth.

Even though they had taken two hours of ballet class together in the adjoining room, decorum dictated that professional star and college student inhabit opposite ends of the studio; they barely let their eyes meet. But when his glance wandered in her direction the electricity in the room crackled like wildfire and even Madame would start to feel uncomfortable. Irritated, she'd glance at Gelsy, only to see the girl's eyes firmly locked on the floor.

But class was over now, and Monsieur had promised him they would all have lunch together and speak in nothing but French! How happy he was not to try and struggle with the horribly slippery English. Forever he made silly mistakes and reporters (always women or gay men) would giggle and say how "cute" he was. Of all the words in the language, "cute" was the one he dreaded the most. It was associated with "petite" in his mind, and being reminded of the short stature that was his Achilles heel.

Not being tall in ordinary life where women wear heels occasionally is one thing, he thought. In the ballet where they are always on their toes and towering over you, it is quite another. But this Gelsy! So tiny, and such small feet! On her toes she barely came to his cheek, and he loved being able to see over her head. That she was stunningly beautiful and danced with truly professional ease made her the perfect partner for him. He just couldn't understand why such a dancer would want a college degree.

They sat down to lunch, the dancers swaddled in layers of knitted woolens to keep their muscles warm for the rehearsal to follow. The conversation flowed in French as smoothly as the red wine Monsieur had been so kind as to provide. When asked what she'd been "up to" lately, Gelsy replied shyly that perhaps a toast would not be out of place, given the time and the circumstances. She had just become engaged and at that moment her fiancé was out shopping for a ring. Smiling, they all raised their glasses to her and David.

Perhaps there was worse news Naj could have received that day, but outside of a horrible accident making it impossible for him to dance again he couldn't imagine what it could have been. Suddenly it occurred to him that this was the woman he'd wanted in his life forever. That he could see himself buying a ring… the rarest, most expensive ring in the world… for her. And now he was too late. He could barely maintain his cool, professional smile.

-25-

David didn't have the slightest doubt it was *the* ring. He'd gone to the campus jewelry store only because he had so little time and knew nowhere else to go. He told the old man at the counter of his situation and brought out his pathetic bank book. He was lucky, there had been a trade-in, the man said. A student had inherited some vintage jewelry she had no use for and wanted to exchange it for a class ring. Ever-helpful to student need, he'd taken two necklaces and the ring.

The ring. Would the gentleman be interested in an emerald-cut garnet set in antique gold, surrounded by tiny diamond chips? He brought it out and it glowed like old wine. David produced the paper circle and it nestled inside the gold band as if there needed to be a final declaration from on high.

He was late getting back to dinner. Robert let him out at the door and then buzzed off for an appointment with his lawyers about the adoption. David used his brand-new side door key to slip in and breeze into the kitchen. Everyone was sitting and eating already, so he grabbed a plate and served himself, brushing by Gelsy on his way to the table and dropping a tiny box next to her wineglass. She was so engrossed in telling Mama about the day's rehearsal that Donald had to tap her elbow twice to get her attention, but when he did the gasp had the desired effect.

The ring was exactly what she'd always wanted, David was a magician and he glowed under all the praise. He slipped it onto her finger and it looked even more beautiful there, as if it just been waiting for the perfect hand to grace. Tears ran down Gelsy's cheek and she said it was the happiest moment of her life. David silently seconded the notion.

That night David made sure to put pajamas on and crawl into bed before Gelsy came into the room. He just wanted to watch her get ready, see her flit around the room and admire the ring on her finger. *His* ring. He'd never felt such a thrill, was so grateful she loved it and thankful he'd been able to afford it. Now he had a reason to feel connected to her, beyond just the sex. He'd given her a ring; tomorrow they'd go to Mass together. It was all beginning to feel real.

"You OK, Davey?" she called from the vanity table, where she was rubbing lotion on her sore feet.

"Sure. Bring the lotion over here and I'll do that for you," he motioned for her to come over to the bed. "You must be half-dead. Tell me everything I missed by coming in late."

She happily hopped on the bed and handed him the bottle, stretching herself out like a python and wiggling her toes at him.

"Nothing exciting. We had lunch, then we rehearsed for two and a half hours. Naj dances completely different from Rennie, of course, but when it comes to lifting me it's pretty much all the same. Oh, I did announce our engagement during lunch and they all toasted us with red wine! I don't really think Naj was too happy about it, though." She made a wry face. "But at least he didn't drop me."

David growled harshly, "He damn well better not," as he gently massaged her bruised toes.

Sex that night was gentle. David knew she was tired and in pain, but nothing could stop him from wanting her. In the morning she was recovered enough to wake him in a most unusual fashion, and David was amused as well as aroused. She seemed to take as much pleasure from exploring his body as he did hers. They decided to conserve water that day by sharing a shower, then race to see who could be dressed for church first. Gelsy won, of course. The girl could slip in and out of her clothes like a reptile shedding its skin, David thought as he watched her whip on a pair of pantyhose.

Ready with at least thirty seconds to spare, the newest couple met the older couple on the landing and all four joyfully piled into Donald's van for the ride to Mass. When they got there and met Robert, heads turned and conversations died down, then started up again in more hushed, rapid-fire patterns. "Who is he?" was the only distinguishable comment, but then, "The ring! Look at her ring!" became a close second.

-26-

After Mass the Monsignor was kind enough to meet with them in private. Donald had called ahead and explained the entire situation so he simply needed an introduction to the new member of the family.

"But I know who you are!" Monsignor exclaimed. "I've seen you sneaking into the old organ loft every Sunday for weeks now! Why did you never come sit with the family before?"

All the others turned to David to gasp. "You did *what*?" Gelsy whispered.

David flushed. "I wanted to hear Gelsy sing, but then I got interested and stuck around."

"Well, we're going to take that into consideration, David. God was obviously speaking to you through Gelsy."

David thought, then nodded agreement. "He's been doing that a lot, lately."

The Monsignor leaned back in his chair. "You know we have RCIA for adults who are searching for answers, but I think you've found your path to the church already, David. And we have much more leeway these days. Come with me out to the courtyard and let's talk a few minutes, man to man." He got up, opened a side door and quickly ushered David out to a small patio area.

The other four sat in deep conversation of how the legal proceedings to make David a Chaveral were going (excellent) and how soon the couple should be married ("asap" said the bride-to-be) when the Monsignor opened the door, ushered David in and surprisingly announced, "OK, everyone, he's now a Catholic."

As the office door closed behind them on the way out all anyone could say was "What happened out there?" David just looked mysterious, smiled and said, "Monsignor said I can't tell anybody. Seems I came in the church by the back door."

In bed that night, Gelsy wanted to know more.

"Honestly, there's not much to tell. I came originally from an orphanage ran by Sisters so he knew I'd been baptized. I just got a quick run-through on everything else, made confession and ate a wafer."

"Made confession! Aha!!" She gloated "And I wasn't a fly on the wall for *THAT* one!"

David chuckled and turned her around to face him. "There's nothing there you don't already know, Gelsy. If you think there is, ask me and I'll tell you."

"No, my love, because a man should have some privacy." She kissed him sweetly on the tip of his nose. "But if you remember any wild escapade you do want to share, feel free. I'm not likely to have any of my own, you know."

"Poor baby girl. Am I cutting you off too soon? Eighteen, that's pretty young." He thoughtfully stroked her soft, wavy hair.

"I have everything I want, thank you very much. I have no need for escapades at this stage of the game."

"I'm nearly ten years older than you are, Gelsy. You'll get bored quickly with me and want somebody your own age." He was giving voice to his worse fear now, and he had to take his hand from her hair so she wouldn't see it shake.

She drew back a little and looked at him, ran her fingers over the soft fur on his chest, admired the straight shoulders with their knotted packs of muscle. She traced his nipples with her fingertips and said, "Nooo, *mon Cherie*, I think it will take me an entire lifetime just to explore and appreciate you properly." And here she began to kiss his nipples, his chest, and work her way downwards as David nearly lost consciousness in the pure joy of her kisses.

Later, watching her sleep, David tried to process it all. How unbearably thrilling it was to be next to her in bed. How unbelievable that he'd just made love to her. Of course he still couldn't fully enter her; that might take a very long time. She was so tiny he had to always be aware he might be causing her pain. When he did, she would never admit it but he could feel the spasms that came automatically, and he learned to pull back. He'd hold and kiss her until she was calmed. Learning to love her like this was like learning a new language, and, God, he loved her so much!

He put his head back on the pillow and tried to close his eyes. How could he sleep now? She made him feel so proud and so helpless, all at the same time. He didn't know a man could feel like that.

A car was driving up. After dinner Donald had been scheduled to give a lecture-demonstration for a charity function, and was probably just now getting home. David silently eased out of the bed and into his pajamas and robe. He'd go down and greet his future father-in-law.

Donald came in looking like he'd had a hard night. These charity functions required a person to be both professor and performer, and to be top-notch for both. Keeping the show going all evening had been tough; seeing David with a shot of whiskey in his hand put a huge grin on his face.

"Thought you might need this," David said, toasting him with a salute before downing his shot.

"My boy, you couldn't be more right!" Donald exclaimed, downing his and flopping onto the sofa. "This was one for the books. Pour me another, please," and he held out his glass.

David obliged, poured another one for himself and settled in next to him.

"Trouble sleeping?" Donald became a concerned parent to his new son.

"A little. Still seems so strange," said David, sighing, "I'm afraid if I sleep, I'll wake up and she'll be gone."

Donald nodded his head approvingly, "That just shows she's got you good! Her mom did the same thing to me, son. I'll never forget the feeling. My lord, I didn't know if I was coming or going for weeks after we met… months! Well, hell… years! She's still got me tied around her little finger. Get ready for a long ride, David."

"So you're saying… ?"

"Learn to sleep next to her. Pretty soon, you won't be able to sleep if she's *not* there!" He tossed back the last of his drink, winked at David and bounded down the opposite hallway.

-27-

Robert came by to pick him up early the next morning, which meant he had to leave her sleeping. That was harder than he expected, but somehow he forced himself not to disturb the lovely sight of her, curled up like a kitten with a face half-buried in a pillow. David wasn't the kind of guy to write notes, but he left one that morning. "Hate to leave – see you soon" was what it said, but it was all he could do to not even touch her hair when he left it on his pillow.

She came in for class that morning grinning and holding the folded note in her hand, so excited she could barely look at him. Gelsy was always a happy presence in the room, but today she completely overwhelmed her fellow students with her good humor. Their Monday blues had no defense against her insistence of joy. Only with Robert's entrance did they all take their seats and try to pretend they were students again.

Gelsy still sat in the same place immediately in front of Robert's huge desk, although a regular desk had by now been found for her. David, as always, stood behind Robert's desk, leaning on the whiteboard and watching Robert for any instructions that might come from this impulsive instructor. One never knew when he might decide on an immediate demonstration.

And so as he stood waiting, with his body in the same ready-for-action mode he'd acquired in the military, he suddenly noticed Gelsy's demeanor had changed. Her bubbliness was gone and she was forcing an interest in the lecture she obviously didn't feel. A number 2 pencil was in her hand, being wound in and out of her fingers as if she were braiding rope. Then David realized it was because she was watching him out of the corner of her eye, and becoming more restless by the minute. She picked up the note he'd left for her and read it several times, each time with a sad look as if she imagined waking up in the empty bedroom to find it on his pillow, and then looked at him while pretending to study the poster of elements over his head.

David watched as she pressed her side against the back of her desk as if deliberately creating sensation and then understood… she needed him! She woke up to find him gone and seeing him now made her realize she was used to having him there in the morning. He wasn't the only one who felt disappointed at missing their time together.

At that moment her number two pencil snapped with a sharp *twang*. Looking at David's shoulders under his lab coat, she had clenched her fist and the pencil had broken from the strain. Luckily, it happened as Robert's voice had risen to make a point and the other students had opened there notebooks. Only David heard the snap and saw Gelsy sitting there, now trying desperately to write while holding two pieces of a broken pencil together.

Unfortunately, the piece with the lead was the smaller of the two pieces and she was having such a deliciously difficult time that David was nearly shaking with laughter. As calmly as possible, he opened Robert's desk drawer a few inches, took out a newly-sharpened pencil, took two of his long strides to stand next to Gelsy. Silently he replaced the broken pencil, gave a quick nod to Robert that he was leaving for a moment and stepped out to the men's restroom.

There he tossed the broken pieces in a trashcan and laughed until he could barely stand up.

The next day was his therapy session. *Man, will I have a lot to tell the jarhead!* David mused to himself on the walk over to Student Health. Climbing the stair, a trip he never made without first checking to be sure no one from any of his classes saw him headed to the mental health unit, he began to get anxious. *How much should I tell him, anyway?*

The door leading to the ex-Marine's office was open. David popped his head in and was immediately motioned inside. Marvin, his therapist, was filing some notes and looked relieved to see him. "I've had a feeling all day, David, that if you showed up this morning it was going to be a great day. How about it... ready for any breakthroughs?"

"You know what they say, Marv, beware of what you wish for. You just might get it."

The stocky little man, only slightly older than David, thoughtfully walked back to his desk. "Sounds like you have something for me. Care to sit down and spill it?"

David took the seat offered and leaned forward until he was leaning on the desk. "Suppose I told you I'm in love?"

"I'd say hallelujah and who's the lucky young lady?"

"Gelsy Grandwood, daughter of the head of the music department and my professor's god-daughter."

Not *the* Gelsy, the dancer? Oh, my boy, we need to talk about this..."

"Save your warnings, Doc. I love her, she loves me, we're engaged, end of story."

"I knew I should have insisted on medication, David. I'm seriously worried now about hallucinations."

"If you don't believe me, feel free to contact her parents, Robert, or the priest who just converted me to Catholicism so I can marry her in the Church."

"Whoa! Either you've been indulging in some cracker-jack drugs or you really have gotten yourself the top catch at UCSM. I'm thinking maybe I should give up and just congratulate you after all."

David gave him one of his rare half-wistful smiles. "That would be nice, but don't let it stand in your professional way.

Good news doesn't come easy to me, Doc, and I'm having a helluva time dealing with this. It doesn't seem right, somehow. I can't accept it."

"It's going to mean a big change in your life, David. From what I know about you, you've been pretty much a loner."

A loner! Yeah, that's what he'd been, before Randy. He sank back in the chair, put his head in his hands and started remembering…

He remembered being a kid off the streets, a raw recruit in boot camp and meeting the guy who was his same age but seemed so much older. Randy wasn't any older. Heck, like David, he'd lied about his age to get into the army a full year early, it was just that Randy had been born with no fear of anything! When he saw how wary David was of every little thing ("Yeah, Rand, but what if they find out…, Suppose they…") he promptly decided David needed a Big Brother and took over the role.

Never mind that in reality he was 4 months younger than David, he considered himself the senior member of the partnership for several reasons; (1) he could lie and have no fear of being caught, therefore seldom was, (2) he had lost his virginity years ago and what did David mean, he'd never been with a woman?, and (3) he was never scared. He figured he wasn't going to die until it was his time so there was no sense in worrying about it beforehand, combat duty or no combat duty.

The two formed a union they would refer to as the "3Ds" (for "Drunk & Disorderly Duo") and for the next three years, facing down drill sergeants together, enduring boot camp and combat duty, sharing R&R, cigarettes and whatever else they had. Neither had much, since both were street boys with nobody at home to send them nice letters and cookies, like the other recruits, so they made the best of roll call by occasionally sending each other something. A mail-order cake-in-a-can that they could both feast on together, a carton of cigarettes to share, a subscription to a girlie magazine that had every other guy in the platoon knocking on the door. Hell, Randy even dragged him to his first whorehouse.

Somehow they managed to keep each other afloat through two soul-sucking tours of duty, then just before the end of tour two somebody made a mistake. Somebody on their own side. A rocket was launched accidently while their platoon was out on a field search; one minute Randy was walking within six feet of David and the next minute he didn't seem to exist. David remembered trying to call out to him, but there was a cloud around him now and he was in the air. When he came back to the ground with a resounding *thump*, he could see Randy laying in a stream of blood and forced his own broken body over to him. For several minutes, as alarms sounded and medics ran to them, David held what was left of Randy, begging him to put himself back together again, saying, "I love you, man" until a medic pried him loose and stuck a needle in his arm. Slowly everything melted away.

When he woke up it was in a field hospital, with various tubes attaching him to bags and machines. Coolly and methodically he tried to rip them all out. Nurses came running and again he felt a shot that put him back under. When he awoke the next time, his hands were strapped to the sides of the bed.

They put him back together that time, nursed him back to health, then sent him back out for that third tour of duty. "Big mistake," David thought wryly. He was already half-dead inside. Nobody asked him if he wanted to talk to a therapist about his best friend being killed or about nearly dying himself. Nobody asked him if he felt suicidal. (He did.) Back he went, trained this time as a sniper.

In his new unit he found a group of guys who swore they'd found the answer to the long, lonely days and searing nightmares, and its name was heroin. He tried it and he liked it. It kept him from killing himself whenever he thought of Randy, laying there in pieces on the ground.

But it came at a price. By this time he'd also discovered he had an aptitude for studying. To while away the endless hours in the field or in the hospital he'd taken the courses he needed to fill out the gaps in his education and discovered an interest in science. Deciding to do it "just for fun," he began signing up for all the science courses he could take through the military's correspondence courses and, whenever he was on a base for any length of time, he'd try for actual classroom units. Now, nearing the end of his third tour and the end of his active service he realized he had nearly enough credits for a degree.

Unfortunately, he found he had something else, too, a monkey on his back. And if he thought it was a secret, he was soon proven wrong. Called one morning into the conference for top brass only, he had a series of photographs spread out in front of him showing the different transferences of drugs among men in his company. Consideration was going to be taken, he was told, because of his service record, war wounds and opportunities to better himself with his future college plans. Although he was clearly shown to be an active part of this drug ring, if he would agree to give evidence against the others, he could plead guilty but ask for leniency because of his war wounds that were never properly addressed. After a stay in a military rehab hospital, he would be able to take an honorable discharge and get on with his life.

It was what Randy would have wanted him to do, the chaplain told him. Otherwise two lives would have been lost. If he would take the only positive choice and give evidence, someday he might be able to do great things and he could give credit to Randy. It might be the only way to keep his name alive.

That was the reason. David didn't think he could bring himself to turn evidence against men who had been his buddies, doing the same thing he was doing, but he could do it for Randy. It was the only thing that made sense to him, the only thought that kept him going in the long, lonely nights of studying and isolation.

And then another person came into his life; Gelsy. She was alive and could touch him, afraid as he was of being touched again by another human being. She could laugh and talk with him in a strangely personal way, like Randy had done, making him feel like they'd known each other forever.

But Gelsy was young and beautiful. What was she doing with him? In ten years would she regret turning her life over so soon to an older guy who everyone thought of as a *loner...* battle-scarred, with PTSD?

Marvin had listened to all of this without saying a word. Now he leaned across the desk and said, "This girl loves you and wants to spend her life with you. Nothing I've ever heard about her would make me think she's not being sincere, David. If I were you I'd try to bury the past, for her sake. And now I'm going to throw you out because your time is up. Come back next week and tell me about all the wedding plans the two of you have been making!"

Leaving the mental health offices, David again checked both corridors before stepping out. Rounding the corner and descending the stairs he was finally lost in a stream of regular health-care students, one of whom had attached themselves to his back belt loop. Feeling himself slowed down, David tried to turn around to see who it was, but whoever it was stayed directly in back of him and it took three turns before he finally got a glimpse of long flying hair and heard Gelsy's unmistakable giggling.

"Come out of there, you little hermit crab," David grumbled good-naturedly. "And what are you doing here anyway?

"I had to get my B12 shot. And you? Did you see your therapist?"

"Yes, and left him in a dead faint. I hope somebody's come to pour water on him by now."

"Oh good, you told him you're getting married! You must give me his name so he can be invited."

David looked down at her fondly. "Strange, the last thing he said was next week we'd talk about wedding plans. I thought it was premature. Obviously I didn't figure on how fast you and your mom could whip up a wedding."

She slipped her arm through his in preparation to walk him back to the chemistry building and replied pertly, "Darling, the day after the benefit performance is Sunday and we start planning the wedding right after Mass. If you think I'm going to let you slip away from me, you're just downright crazy!"

And so the last weeks ran by as both of them fell into a routine; togetherness and apartness.

Gelsy still had her benefit night performance rehearsals and David had both his own class load in addition to his teaching duties, but they had their classes together, the hoot and weekend nights. Before they knew it, the performance date was in sight, scheduled for the Saturday after a hoot that landed on Adele's birthday. Gelsy was torn; obviously she'd have dress rehearsal all day and night. Would she be able to get away for even an hour?

Cuddled in bed David tried to calm her. "Your mom knows how important this is to you and she'll have another birthday next year. Just remember that your best present to her will be to dance Juliet." He hugged her tightly whenever she whined or worried until she could smile again and think of how happy she'd make her parents with this performance.

"But if it *is* a success, what then?" He couldn't keep the note of anxiety out of his voice.

"What then... do you mean, will I want to go back to New York?"

He stroked her hair and face the way he always did when he lay next to her, not wanting to sleep until he'd filled his mind with images of her beauty. "Yes, my love. Once I get my doctorate I'm sure I could get a job in a research lab in New York, or maybe teach on one of the universities."

She smiled at the thought. "Thank you for considering it, darling. You're right, I like the idea of having a chance to dance the great classic ballets. When I was a little girl I dreamed of being the Swan Queen, what little ballerina doesn't? But eventually I see myself coming back here, you know. I think my greatest dream is to be the head of UCSM's dance department and teach, maybe even someday teach our children! What greater dream could I have than that?"

He gathered her into his arms and buried his face in her hair, kissing her shoulders to keep from crying. For some reason whenever she talked about having children with him, it cut like a knife. His love for her would increase so rapidly his heart couldn't hold it all.

They'd arranged that David would stay in his dorm room for the nights leading up to the benefit. Robert scheduled a series of all-out research projects that would need round-the-clock monitoring. He and David, Gordie and Mark would spell each other analyzing the results as they came in.

The first night wasn't so bad. David was exhausted enough to hit his dorm bed and fall asleep immediately. The second night was worse. There were two Gelsy-less nights ahead of him and he didn't know how he'd make it, but it was the hoot and Adele's birthday. He'd try to be present for the evening because it was very likely Gelsy wouldn't be able to put in any kind of appearance.

He and Robert arrived at the regular time, but it seemed as if the company was cut in half instead of lacking only one member. They were all keenly aware of what a force Gelsy was in the hoot, with her sparkling presence, her playing, singing and jokes. Her youth made them all feel so much younger; without her they felt old and out of spirits.

"It's sad when a woman has to bake her own birthday cake, Adele," David said as she slid the cake pans into the oven.

"No, no, Davey. I make my own favorite, banana cream with chocolate, like I make for you," Adele laughed. "And maybe we still hope she comes."

They had dinner, reassembled on the patio while Adele turned the cake tiers out to cool and got the frosting ready, and then were just tuning up when they heard an unmistakable voice singing, "Happy Birthday to You." From the house Gelsy came with the cake, iced and with candles lit. No one had heard her drive up. It was as if she'd appeared by magic.

"I had Monsieur drop me off beyond the driveway and snuck in so you wouldn't hear me," she explained, while they all joyfully gorged themselves on cake. "I could guess when Mama would have the cake ready to be frosted, and I was right on the button!" She was so pleased with herself, she wiggled all over and took a huge bite of cake. Frosting dotted her nose and David leaned over to kiss it off as everyone laughed.

"You are a woman of many talents, Gelsy Grandwood. I'm proud to have you as a god-daughter," Robert smiled.

Too soon, though, it was time to go; Gelsy was so tired she was nearly asleep on her feet. The extra helping of cake had done its best to give her a short sugar-high but sheer exhaustion had finally claimed her. David took pity and said, "Girl, you need some rest. Robert and I had better head out so you can get to bed."

"Without you. How dull." Curling up in his lap, she tucked her chin into his shoulder and began to drift off.

"Hold on, honey." With no apparent effort, he scooped her up in his arms and marched her up to her bedroom. Stretching her out on her bed, fully clothed, he laid down a moment beside her and said, "Tomorrow is your big day."

"Um-hmmm."

"And no matter what happens, I'll be very proud of you."

"Um-hmmm."

"And after that, you're all mine!"

"*Um-hmmm!!!*"

He kissed her very gently and tiptoed from the room.

"So, this is what love is all about," he whispered to himself, peeking back at her.

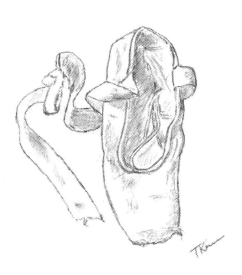

-28-

David stood waiting for Robert to pick him up when Mark and Gordie left the building for the performance. "Why are you waiting for a ride, anyway?" Mark reasoned. "The theater is only a quarter mile away. It's easier to walk."

"I know, but Robert is driving over from his house and I want to go in with him. Besides, there's always the last-ditch chance I'll get invited to Naj's after-performance party." David put on a noble face of optimism.

"Yeah, he wants you there like he wants the KGB on his tail again," Gordie laughed. "Good luck, sucker."

Robert drove up exactly one minute later. "Are we all ready for tonight?" he asked.

"I'm nervous as a cat in a dog run," David replied. "What if something bad happens? What if Naj drops her on purpose just to mess up her big night?"

"First of all, Naj would never do that because it would be *his* reputation on the line. Second, Gelsy herself told me when she was a little girl and I was attending her first recitals, 'Buba, don't worry if I screw up', and yes, she said 'screw up' even back then; 'Because I'm only human and things will happen,' so you see what kind of woman you're dealing with."

David rocked with laughter, "Looks fragile but tough as nails, I know." He calmed down quickly. "Have I mentioned to you lately, Robert, how much in love with her I am?"

"My boy, you don't have to. It's written in big letters on your forehead."

They parked the car about as far away from the theater as the dorm would have been and helped themselves to programs on the way in. Robert, of course, had his seats reserved and did not wait for an usher. Adele and Donald

115

were already seated. Plopping down casually next to them, Robert queried, "Are we all ready for this?"

A resounding "No," surprised David. Robert looked over his shoulder at his and mouthed "Naj."

The performance began. It was actually a long evening of dance, of which the balcony scene would only be the finale. First there were many selections from the various classes and of these Gelsy was in three; the ballet, flamenco and modern. In the first act she danced with the other advanced ballet class members in a scene from "Sleeping Beauty", and for the modern class David had the pure joy of seeing her perform the violin solo he'd seen her first dance from his nest. Looking at his program, he say in was called Canon in D and he thought he'd always remember her in that music.

They four of them spent the intermission drinking wine, eating home-made cookies (it was all for a good cause) and discussing the first act. The others were amazed to hear David had seen the Canon danced before he even knew who Gelsy was, but, as Robert said, it shows what was meant to be.

They went back to their seats and the second act opened with a wild Spanish scene from "Carmen" by the flamenco class. Although Rennie's fancy footwork was lacking, the other men did very well and Luisa made a beautiful Carmen. (Gelsy had flatly refused the role.)

Suddenly the tap and jazz numbers were over and there was a long moment of backstage rearrangement, then it was time. The curtain went up on a bare stage; bare except for a curving stairway leading to a tiny, railed balcony half-hidden in the shadows stage left. As the lights came up Gelsy seemed to float from nowhere onto this little platform, wearing a sheer white muslin nightgown over pink tights and toe-shoes. Her hair was partially braided back, and a few tiny, white blossoms were woven into the braids. A spotlight hit as she put her hand on the rail, leaned out to look over the stage, and David's heart broke. He let out an audible gasp. Robert's hand closed over his.

From stage right came a caped figure. Naj, wearing black tights and velveteen tunic over a white muslin shirt, a long black cape thrown over his right shoulder and trailing on the floor behind him. He circled the stage, as a hound circles for a scent, then came to rest under the balcony.

Juliet was startled; she had seen something, but what? She looked from both sides of her balcony as Romeo made his way slowly out to center stage, letting his cape fall to the ground.

This was the first time David had been able to observe the Russian up close and in action. He'd heard the stories, mostly from Gordie, about his height and reputation with women, so it was time to run his own analysis.

"That Russian" as Robert called him, was rather short, maybe about five foot nine on a good day, but his body was so perfect his height seemed secondary. Every muscle perfectly developed and in its proper place, a mop of golden blonde hair, and an angelic face made him look – at least under stage lights – like an answer to any maiden's prayer. No wonder he'd worked his way down a list of famous women.

"But Gelsy isn't on his list," David had to remind himself. The Russian had missed out on one prize.

Onstage Romeo had turned to show himself to Juliet. Delighted, she rushes down the long flight of stairs to find him in the garden below, missing him, at last finding him, then walking with him. Their love story tells itself in the dance, how they pledge themselves to each other, then, alarmed by the outside world, part until they can meet again to marry. The final tableau of the lovers straining to touch one final time brought tears to David's eyes.

"I've never seen it danced so beautifully," a woman ahead of them said to her escort. "Nor I," thought David. "And I've seen it danced in my mind a thousand times." A feeling of relief swept over him that it was over and could not have gone better; Gelsy *was* Juliet, in all her young, eager hunger for love. And David knew he'd helped her find that part of Juliet; it made him feel incredibly happy to think that.

They fought the crowd like salmon finding their way upstream and soon found the door to the wings. Gelsy and Naj were still standing on the stage, surrounded by admirers. Reporters had already made their way back and were preparing to set up shop, smelling a good story between the world-famous Russian dancer and the budding ballerina.

Adele braved them all to throw herself into Gelsy's arms, and they followed her lead. "*Mon infant*," she blubbered like a baby, "I am so proud. I have no English, and your Papa says I must not speak French in front of the reporters. But I am so proud."

Here her Papa took possession. Between him and Robert, the two men reminded her of every recital they'd attended that got her to this point, and how bursting with pride they were. When they'd slowed the barrage of embraces, she turned and searched out David, standing uncertainly behind everyone in the crowd. One quick step, a jump, and she was in his arms. He had no words in French or English for her, only, "Girl, girl…" and then his lips on hers.

It was enough for the reporters. Naj's head had snapped around at the sudden abandonment of his partner, and between the look on his face in the background as the two lovers embraced one could easily read the next day's headlines, "Her REAL Romeo!"

David thought about none of that, cared for none of them right now. His girl was back in his arms where she belonged. He wanted to carry her off, but he knew she still had the obligation of attending the benefit dinner. He'd have to let her go again, but just for a little while. When they came back together again it would be for good. Tomorrow after Mass they'd start planning the wedding.

"*Mon Cherie*, I must take you to your dressing room and help you get ready for the dinner." Adele was gently trying to pry Gelsy off David's chest, where she was clinging like a little girl lost. David took her shoulders, kissed the top of her head and said, "Go with Mama. I'll see you soon," and she gave a tired smile before trotting off with her adoring mother.

Robert came up and put his hand on David's back, encouraging him to walk toward the wing exit without looking back. "Let's hit the road, my boy," he said, with obvious glee in his voice. "I do believe we've worn out our welcome here. Naj pointedly invited Donnie and Adele to his party and just as pointedly ignored us! Well, we know when we're not wanted"

By now they were out in the open air and headed to the car. Robert chortled, "He knows he has Gelsy's company for tonight and that's the end of it! You'll have her for the rest of her life."

-29-

Gordie and Mark were waiting in the lobby for him at Melville. Saturday nights found the dorm pretty much deserted, there were too many parties and events to leave even the loneliest nerd stranded. This evening at the end of a quarter the two lone inhabitants didn't even try to disguise the ice-cold six-pack of beer between them. "We've been waiting," Gordie smirked. "Didn't think you had a rat's ass chance of getting inviting to the shindig." With that he broke open the pack and began passing out cans.

"Afraid I'm not good enough for such distinguished company," David half-mockingly replied, taking the offered can and seating himself. "I'm not on Naj's buddy list right now."

"We were in the back of the stage and saw the whole thing," Mark answered. We watched the show from the wings. Luisa got us in."

"Wow, you guys had a better seat than I did!"

"For a lot of stuff you didn't see," Gordie replied. "Like how much Naj was trying to play Romeo *off*-stage as well as on." He watched the shadow pass over David's face. "And how much extra energy Gelsy used up trying to keep out of his reach." The shadow dissipated and David took a long swig from his can. "So tell us, David. We've been pretty patient, but it's easy to see she's been wearing a new ring. Did you get it for her?"

David hung his head. He'd been dreading this conversation. All the nights he'd spent away from the dorm, Gordie must have noticed. And the way Gelsy acted around him now. She tried hard not to be seen in class, but Gordie knew her so well, and every time she looked at David her heart was in her eyes.

"Yeah, I bought her the ring."

"Are you two engaged?"

Silence. How much could he tell them? They were his only friends, but they also worked for Robert. David figured they were going to find out pretty soon anyway.

"We're planning the wedding tomorrow after Mass." That had the effect of a thunderbolt. Both young men sat up straight, looked at each other, then tried to choke out congratulations. "Wait, there's more I think you should know. Robert wants me to take his name."

Now he had them sitting back in their seats, barely able to move. "You guys probably don't know, but I'm an orphan who ran away from a foster family to join the army, so my last name doesn't mean anything to me. Robert wants to adopt me, and then Gelsy will have his name when she marries me."

For a minute you could have heard a pin drop. Mark was silent but Gordie's face was twisted in an expression almost of horror. David frankly felt sorry for him. It would have been his dream scenario.

Mark broke the silence with, "I hate to be a Philistine, but do you have any idea how rich you're going to be on the day you become Chaveral's son?"

"Rich? What do you mean, rich?" David was baffled.

"My young innocent, I speak as the son of an accountant who sometimes does work for Chaveral's lawyer. He is worth millions."

"You've got to be kidding me," David was in no mood for this kind of game.

"No, no, listen to me. Besides all the money he makes here as one of the highest-paid professors on staff, he also holds several patents on the results of his research projects." (David did know about the patents, but never thought of them making money.) "He has no wife or children, spends very little on himself, has made some amazingly good investments over the years, and Gelsy is his sole heir. Well, now you," Mark toasted him with his can of beer. "How happy I am to have friends like this!"

David could not have been more astonished.

Later, when he was in his room, there was a knock at the door. Gordie came in with "Is it OK if we talk?"

David motioned him over to the only chair while he sat on the edge of the unmade bed.

"Listen, David, I didn't want to talk about this in front of Mark, but I couldn't help noticing you've stayed out all night lots of times lately. Were you with… her?"

David hung his head. "After we told her folks, Donald said I could stay over sometimes if I wanted – that there was no shame. He and Adele lived together before they were married."

Gordie was beaten but unbowed. "I see. She must love you very much, David."

"Gordie, you have no idea how much I love her!"

"She deserves nothing less. You'd better worship her, take care of her, or you know I'll come take you out." And here he managed a weak smile.

"I know how you feel about her, Gord. Don't worry."

There was a brief silence.

"Tell me, if you can David," Gordie was hesitant, "What's it like?"

"What do you mean, Gordie?"

Gordie fidgeted. "I've never been with anybody. Mark keeps telling me to go pick up a girl, you know, but I don't know how and I'm not sure that's what I really want to do, anyway." Here he stopped, looking miserable.

"Listen, if you're talking about a hooker, I've been there and I'll tell you it's not what you want."

"Well, what do I do? I don't think anybody's ever going to want me, David, seriously. And I want to know what it's like."

David thought about this, trying to put himself in Gordie's place. "I can tell you that it's the craziest, most soul-searing thing to ever happen to you, when it's with somebody you love. When it's with somebody you pay, you feel a quick high, then you're depressed. No comparison. If I'd known the difference, I'd have skipped the whores, Gordie. I wish I'd kept myself completely for Gelsy, even though she says 'one of us had to know what they were doing," and he gave a bitter laugh, twisting around on the bed as if he were looking for her.

Gordie nodded gravely. "I understand. When my dad went away into the Marines, before I was born, he ended up going to girls even though he and my mom were already married. He said he just got so damned lonely for a woman, but later he was sorry. It wasn't worth it."

"But you can't ever judge anybody, Gordie. It's a hell of a feeling. I've done drugs, and heroin is the only thing that comes close. You feeling hungry for it in a way you can't describe, so don't ever pass judgment."

"No, I don't blame my dad. And I don't think I want to try it because I might like it enough to spend money on it. But I wish I knew there was somebody out there who'd just love me and let me love her."

David looked at him with deep compassion. "And I want that for you, too, Gordie. I really do."

-30-

Gordie had been gone about an hour and David had dozed off on the bed without undressing when the phone rang. It was Robert's voice, but so choked up David at first had a hard time making it out.

"Get downstairs. I'll pick you up in five minutes."

"Whoa, what's…"

"Five minutes!" Click. The phone was dead. "Oh my God," thought David, "The lab. Something's happened at the lab. What did I do…???" and he ran some cold water to splash on his face, thankful he hadn't changed out of his clothes.

In five minutes he was on the street when Robert's car pulled up. He got in and said, "How bad is it? What did I do, Robert? Did I forget to set the timers? Did the power go off? What happened?"

Robert was silent. Instead of driving, he pulled the car over to the side of the road and gripped the steering wheel without looking at David. "Not the lab, David. Worse, much worse. There's no easy way…" he shuddered. "A drunk driver hit them on their way back from the party. Donnie and Adele are gone. Gelsy's in surgery, but they don't think she's going to make it. That's where we're going right now."

He struggled to get control of himself and put the car back in gear, easing it onto the lane and into the main road that led to the hospital. David sat back like a man hit by a brick. Donald and Adele dead? Not possible. He was talking with them a few hours ago. Gelsy in surgery, maybe dying…."

Here he ran up against a black wall. Nothingness took over and suddenly they were at the hospital, parking in the emergency parking area. David followed Robert like a half-blind man, staggering through the lobby and trying to keep up with the frantic little professor.

"Professor Chaveral!" A woman's voice rang out. Down a hall a young black woman in a nurse's uniform was motioning for them to follow her. "I've been watching for you, sir. You don't remember me, but I was in your class a few years ago. When I heard she was your god-daughter I made it my business to see you were contacted. Come this way." She ushered them into an elevator. "I know what you're going to ask, sir, and all I can tell you is she was in a bad way when I last saw her. They took her right into surgery, and there hasn't been any news since then. She'd lost a lot of blood, I know that much. She was in the back seat and had to be cut out by the firemen."

By this time they'd reached the fifth floor and were half-way down the hall at a surgery waiting area. "I'll have to leave you here. There's coffee over in the corner, help yourself. She's in the operating room just behind this room, and the chapel is right around the corner if you feel the need for prayer. I know I'll be praying for her all night, sir." And with a quick hug, she was gone.

Robert paced the room like an animal in a cage. "David, David, what can I do? Donnie and Adele, my God! I can't begin to deal with that right now. It all has to be about *her*. She has to be saved. What am I going to do if she's gone, too? Oh, my God!" And here he sat on a folding chair with his hands raking through his hair and beard wildly.

David sat down beside him. As if realizing for the first time David was there, Robert turned and put his arms around him. "David, my boy! You must be in agony. How can I be so thoughtless?"

But David was silent, motionless.

Robert tried to force coffee on him, but he seemed like a man lost in another world. Finally Robert said, "My son, I'm going to ask you to do something for me. I have to stay here.

Whatever happens, I have to know immediately. But if you would go for me to the chapel and pray for her, it would make me feel so much better. David, will you do that for me?

Without another sound, David stood and went out into the hall.

-31-

Like most hospital chapels this one was small, with only three sets of tiny pews and a four-by-eight foot raised area at the end to hold the narrow altar. The most remarkable feature was the crucifix hanging behind the altar. It was large, baroque and strangely similar to the one David wore around his neck. In such a tiny, utilitarian chapel it seemed to belong in a cathedral.

David went to the first pew, genuflected and sat down, still as if in a trance. Once here, though, looking at the cross, it made him sit up and think of something. Slowly he pulled out the crucifix from around his neck and, and he did so often whenever he had a problem or a bad day, kissed the spot where Gelsy's lips had been.

It was enough. Now he was awake and in the moment.

His head came down with a crack on the back of the seat as he slumped, suddenly changing into a helpless, raging incarnation of a human being.

This is it, this is the pay-off! was all he could put into words. *The big pay-off for letting me have her, love her, think I was going to marry her.* He brought his head upright.

Donald and Adele! Both gone!! Of course she's with them! I can see that. They're together, right now, a family, like they always were. Whatever made me think I could be part of that family? And now he raged by throwing his body against the carved end of the pew, over and over.

Staggering to his feet, he tried to reach out to touch the crucifix. The raised area around it was only four inches high and he ended up tripping and coming down hard on the left side of the altar. Here he stayed in a semi-fetal position, most of the breath knocked out of him, all he could do was groan. Laying there, he had his first real conversation with God. All the barriers were down and there was no one else to talk to. Memories came flooding back.

God, did you let me have her just to take her away, like you gave me Randy? I can't go through this again. I nearly didn't make it the first time, remember? I had my service revolver in my mouth but you stopped me, or Randy's spirit did. I liked to think it was him, telling me not to be such an idiot, that I was meant for better things. It was his memory that got me through the mess with the drugs in the army. I told Gelsy I'd never said 'I love you' to another living soul, but I never told her I'd said it to a dead one. Is this part of the payback?

His therapist had slowly been bringing him to accept the idea that what he was doing with his life could be for himself, not just a living tribute to a dead friend. Gelsy made him believe his life could have a future that included other people; herself, her family, Robert, maybe someday their own children. He'd been seeing so much more ahead.

She'd made him believe in God; now he raged at God. *Is this some kind of twisted practical joke? Give me the most precious thing I ever could have imagined, then say, "No, changed my mind. I'm taking her back.' Somehow I can see her right now. She's with her parents, isn't she? And they're happy to be together.* Blinking, he stared at the ceiling.

Clearly, he saw the three of them; standing together, holding hands and walking away from him.

Rolling over he slammed his fists into the floor, yelling out loud, "No, *NO*, come back, Gelsy! You begged me not to leave *you*, don't you leave me! *COME BACK!*"

He rolled onto his back to stare at the ceiling again. The vision was gone.

Sitting upright, he looked at his watch. Two fifteen.

What would he do if they came and told him she was dead? Easy, he'd blow his brains out, no problem. First he'd have to be sure she was really gone, though. He'd make them show him the body so he could kiss her one last time. Then, from the minute he stood over her, he'd turn and start running, and counting. One-thousand one, one-thousand two… down five flights of stairs, he looked at his watch, how many seconds? Maybe thirty? Then out the rear exit and past the nursing building.

He checked his watch and counted off another fifteen seconds. To the student union, maybe a minute, across the quad to the science department, another thirty seconds. He'd be running uphill but across the grade, another minute.

Up past the dance department to Melville and up the stairs, thirty more seconds, don't wait for an elevator. Have the key ready, idiot, so you can get right into your room, fifteen seconds. Grab the gun from under the mattress, stuff it in your stupid mouth, take the safety off and pull the trigger... Maybe an extra few seconds if he stopped to pray to her.

He looked back at his watch. Just about three and a half minutes. It was comforting, somehow, to think that after he knew she was dead and kissed her good-bye he'd only have to live another three and a half minutes before joining her.

He crept back to the pew. "Gelsy, You will wait for me, won't you?" he murmured to himself as he sank down. Stretching out full-length, he pillowed his head on his hands and wept.

He must have dozed a little; Gordie was standing over him, shaking his shoulder. "David! Hey man, Chaveral's looking for you," and he started up the chapel aisle. David had to shake himself before standing to follow. He hadn't seen Gordie's expression. Was it good news or bad? "Well," he pulled himself up bleakly, "it doesn't matter. I already know what to do."

Walking into the waiting room he knew it was bad. Robert stood sobbing in the arms of a surgeon whose scrubs were soaked with blood. *Gelsy's blood*, David thought, feeling faint and preparing himself to demand to see her body. Mark was standing behind them, with two cups of coffee in his hands and an unfathomable expression on his face.

Robert turned to David and gasped, "No, my boy, don't look at me like that. She's *ALIVE*!"

That was all. Everything seemed dark and Gordie guided him to a chair. Mark immediately put a cup of hot coffee in his hand and helped him get it to his lips. The doctor sat Robert down, too, and pulled up a chair, himself.

"Yes, she's alive," he said, looking utterly exhausted, "but don't give me the credit. When she came in tonight there was less than a 1 percent chance of her living this long. I did everything, Robert... pulled out my entire bag of magic tricks, but it was no good. She coded out, and we couldn't get her started again. Everybody stepped away from the table and waited for me to call it, and I couldn't! I looked at the time, two fifteen, and couldn't make myself say it."

Here David came back to life and sat bolt upright. *Two fifteen*?!

"I remembered bringing that little girl into the world. You know, Robert, Donnie was so squeamish I couldn't trust him in the delivery room with Adele, but he made me promise I'd time his baby's first gasp for breath so he'd know when she officially entered the world. All I could think of was, I can't call her last breath, too." He bowed his head at the memory.

Robert cried, "What happened, Michael?

"Well, I stood there for at least three minutes, doing CPR and playing with the machines, until one of the nurses stepped up to call it for me. Just then, Gelsy started breathing on her own. *On her own*, Robert! It was a miracle. Nearly three and a half minutes gone, and she suddenly came back!"

Three and a half minutes.

"Gelsy, You will wait for me, won't you?" he'd asked.

Robert was clearly overjoyed but had to ask, "Does the time without oxygen pose any problems for her brain? What about her spinal cord? Will she dance again?"

"Slow down, now. I'm just trying to keep her alive! We're going to move her into an ICU room and monitor her until -- and if – she comes to. Notice I said 'if,' Robert. She may be in a coma. I can't make any promises, not even that she'll still be alive tomorrow."

"Oh, yes, she will. My god-daughter is a fighter! You'll see. Oh, my…" he gasped twice and swayed in the chair. All the color drained from his face as he suddenly slumped forward.

"Nurse!" the doctor called, and promptly put out a Code Blue. The four men in the room stretched Robert out between folding chairs while waiting for a gurney. "Lay still. If you're a good boy, I'll see you get a room right next to your god-daughter, but you are definitely staying here tonight, Robert."

"Ordinarily I'd fight you tooth and nail, Michael, but put me close to Gelsy and I'll do about anything. Say my son can stay and take care of us both and I'll be even less trouble."

"Your son? Since when did you procreate, you old bachelor, you?"

"Since the beginning of the quarter. Michael, meet David Collins-soon-to-be-Chaveral, my TA and very soon to not only be my son but Gelsy's husband."

The doctor looked like he'd been jolted by a live wire. "Oh, my Lord, how did I get left out of the loop like this? Well, congratulations, David. I'm doubly glad we were able to keep her on this planet, but I suspect maybe you had something to do with that. I think she may be fighting to get back to you."

"I hope you're right, sir," David's voice nearly failed him. "Because I'm not ready to let her go."

There was a commotion out in the hallway. The gurney taking Gelsy to her room had just ran into the empty gurney coming for Robert. "Looks like we have a traffic jam out there. I'll get it straightened out."

Robert gestured to Gordie and Mark, handing over the keys to his car. "You fellows take my car out of the emergency parking area before I get a ticket and drive it back to the dorm. To the dorm, mind you – no road trips!" He turned back to David. "I'll assume you'll be staying here?"

"Nothing could make me leave, sir."

"I didn't think so. You get set up in Gelsy's room and report to me if anything happens!"

"I promise, sir." And he was off, following her gurney to the ICU ward. The doctor came back with the gurney for Robert. "Michael, that's a damned good man, there. I hope you'll let him stay with her. He really needs to be there, and I think she needs him, too."

"I think you're probably right, Robert."

-32-

What time was it now? Sometime after 6:00 a.m.? The hospital would be awake and getting ready for breakfast pretty soon. David was as bone-tired as he'd ever been in his life. Sitting in the chair next to Gelsy's bed, he watched her breathe as all the machines whirled and clicked. Luckily, she was breathing on her own and only had a tiny tube of oxygen inserted in one nostril. Outwardly she looked beautiful, only too thin and extremely pale. *The color you see in seashells*, David thought to himself. Was she going to be all right, or would her mind be affected from the lack of oxygen? Would she walk again, let alone dance? *It doesn't matter*, David thought, *Just give her back to me, God, in any way, and let me love her for the rest of my life. I swear, that's all I ask*!

Sighing, he tried to get comfortable in the chair. It was impossible, so he slid down to the floor, pillowed his head on his arm, and drifted off.

He was dreaming he saw a white spider crawling.... No, it was a thin hand on the guardrail. Amazed, he reached up to touch it. The fingers closed around his and he gasped, "*Gelsy!*"

Scrambling to a kneeling position on the floor, he found himself looking into her wide, frightened eyes. He got to his feet, her fingers still holding his as she looked slowly around the room. "You're in the hospital, Gelsy," he whispered to her.

Nodding slightly, she tugged on his fingers and pointed to the bed beside her, and to him. "What's the matter, girl? What do you want?" She continued to point to the space on the bed beside her. "Let me get a nurse," and he reached for the call button.

"No, no," she whispered brokenly now, "Cold, Davey, I'm so cold! Please make me warm!"

He had to laugh, "Gelsy, I can't get in *bed* with you! This is a hospital!!"

"Please," she looked at him with so much love, "I need to feel your heart beat. You need to help me come back, Davey. *I'm not all the way yet.* Please get close to me. Help me come back!"

It was enough. He took in a quick breath, kicked off his shoes, and, carefully lifting the covers, pushed his body as close to hers as possible. Draping the covers over them both, he reached over and scooped her broken body into his chest, trying to hold her as lightly as possible. Her skin was so icy cold it frightened him, but as soon as she felt his body against hers he could feel her relax and start to breathe with him.

Slowly the skin warmed and even turned a little pink. He kissed her forehead, the tears falling straight from his closed eyes into the pillowcase. It was all he could do to keep breathing steadily for her without choking up.

"Davey?"

"Yes, Gelsy"

"Mama and Papa are in heaven."

He flinched. "I know, girl."

"I was with them. I could have stayed. But I saw you calling to me. You asked me to come back."

"I did, Gelsy." He held her closer. "I begged you not to leave me!"

"And Mama and Papa said it was OK for me to come back and live my life with you."

Deep in his heart he thanked God for the miracle of his vision in the chapel. She had seen and heard him. She followed him back. All the time he was planning to go to be with her…

"Davey?"

"Yes, Gelsy."

"I'm warmer, and I love feeling your heart beat."

Now she was unbuttoning his shirt and kissing his bare chest.

"What do you think you're doing, girl?" he whispered.

"I told you I wanted you to warm me up, didn't I? Maybe I just want to know I'm really alive."

"Gelsy, you have a cast on your leg, your whole body is wrapped in bandages, but I can tell you're alive, thank God!" He kissed her gently once, twice, then more fervently.

"*Hhuummmph*!!" The light in the room had suddenly been switched on and the doctor was standing there, an amazed and half-laughing nurse by his side. "My understanding was you two are *engaged* to be married. What are you doing sneaking in bed together when my back is turned?"

"Don't blame Davy," Gelsy spoke up, "I was so cold; I asked him to warm me up."

"Well, you both are looking warm enough now. Might I possibly separate you so I can get some vitals? You, David, might run over and tell Robert his little girl is feeling better."

"Buba is here?!" Gelsy asked, weakly.

"Yes, darling," the doctor said to Gelsy with a grin. "He nearly had a heart attack worrying about you, so I tucked him into bed next door. And if you both are good you may even have breakfast together this morning. Now, about those vitals…" David slowly pushed himself off the bed, after one last kiss to Gelsy's forehead. Once off, he seated himself, put his shoes back on, buttoned his shirt and was out the door with a "Be back soon, girl."

Next door there was the sound of sawing logs. Robert was asleep, but David judged he'd want to be woke up for good news. "Robert," he said, gently shaking him. "Robert, it's David."

"Huh… David? David?!? Is something wrong??!!"

"No, something is right. Gelsy. She's awake and seems to be OK. The doctor is taking her vitals right now, but he said if you're a good boy you can have breakfast with her."

Robert stared into his eyes as if making sure David wasn't telling him a white lie, then began blinking back the tears. "My boy, that's the best news I've ever heard in my whole life."

"You? How about me?! When she woke up and stretched her hand out, it nearly scared the tar out of me. Then the doctor came in and caught us in bed together because she said she was cold and wanted me to warm her up!"

For some reason Robert found this hysterically funny. "Oh, I'm sure Michael didn't appreciate that at all! He's a very strict Baptist, you know, David."

"I found that out the hard way. Well, just thought I'd let you know. I'm sure he'll come over to give you the details himself. I'm going to go back over and make sure she's OK."

As he came through the door, the doctor was saying, "I can't take the credit, young lady, but you seem well on your road to recovery. Is that fiancé of yours studying medicine, by any chance?"

"Sorry, sir," David replied, "I'm hoping to become a biochemist, like Dr. Chaveral."

"Of course, Robert did tell me he's taking you for his son. Congratulations on getting both a fantastic father and a lovely bride-to-be, David. Still, you would have made a great doctor."

"Davey would be wonderful at anything he did, Doctor," Gelsy chirped up for her beloved's abilities. "Buba says he'll win a Nobel someday!"

"Does he? Well, your godfather is seldom wrong, sweet girl, so I'll watch out for this young man. And I'll trust him to stay with you while you're recovering… if he keeps both feet on the floor!"

With that last remark the good doctor took up his clipboard and exited, to Gelsy's giggles under the covers and David's embarrassed flushing.

He had barely closed the door behind him when she whispered, "Davey, come back beside me."

"Get back in bed with you? No way, Gelsy! You heard what he just said, and Robert told me he's hard-core Baptist. I'm not getting us both in trouble with him."

Just then the door opened and he took a quick step away from the bed, but it was the nurse with a sleeping pill for Gelsy. After she took it and the nurse left, the pleading began again, "Please, Davey. Even with the sleeping pill, I know I won't be able to sleep if you're not beside me. Too much has happened and I'm still in a state of shock. I don't want to drift off and not come back again, but if you're lying next to me you'll anchor me to this world."

The thought of her falling asleep and not waking up again was all the persuasion he needed. Once again he kicked off his shoes and eased his way into the hospital bed beside her, being careful not to jar the broken little body. Instead he allowed her to find a way to lean into him. Soon they were side by side, lightly touching at the shoulders and holding hands. Within a few moments she was nodding and soon she was fast asleep. Watching her breathe and holding her hand, David thought there was no way he could sleep that night. He would keep watch over her to make sure she never missed a breath, and he'd never stop feeling her pulse by holding her hand. He was wrong. The strain of the terrible night had drained him more than any mission he'd ever been on during a tour of duty. Sleep took him over as he watched her sleep.

Waking up to see her still sleeping soundly, he had just enough time to ease himself out of bed and put on his shoes before the doctor came through the door on his morning rounds.

"You've been watching over her all night, David? You must be dead tired, son."

"No, sir. I did manage to get a few hours' sleep."

"Well, Robert has called for your friend to come pick you up and take you back to the dorm. No arguments! Gelsy is doing fine, and she has a breakfast date with her godfather, anyway. You need a shower and some undisturbed rest before you come back here, understand?"

David managed a weak smile of obedience. "Yes, sir. Just give me a chance to tell my girl I'm leaving," at this Gelsy had begun to awaken, "and that I'll be back this evening."

Gelsy opened her eyes to take in the two men. "Plotting against me, Doctor?"

"Sending your lover away for his own good, dear girl. The poor lad is half-dead with worry and sleeplessness. He can get some rest and come back tonight. Meanwhile, your Buba is coming in to have breakfast with you in just a few minutes."

Gelsy looked at David with her eyes wide open and said, "You're right, doctor! I've been so selfish, keeping him here. My dearest Davey, you must go back to the dorm and rest. Here, kiss me good-bye," and she held her arms out, even the arm with the needles still attached.

Gently he took her face in his hands and kissed her. "I'll be back before dinner, girl. Don't go anywhere without me, promise."

"I promise," she said meaningfully, looking him straight in the eyes. "I'll be right here waiting for you. Just get some sleep, and sweet dreams, darling."

He stopped at the door to take one last look at her, then nodded, turned and left. It seemed like a long walk down to the emergency exit, but Gordie was waiting in Robert's car just outside the door with the engine idling. It felt good to relax into the seat, close his eyes and let himself be chauffeured back to the dorm.

"How's she doing?" Gordie asked, anxiety in every word.

"She's doing amazingly well, Gordie. You know I couldn't leave her if she weren't."

"I know, David. You must have had the worst time of your life, thinking you were going to lose her."

"Funny, isn't it? I've been afraid of losing her all along, but not in that way. I'm nearly ten years older than she is and up until now my biggest worry was that she'd realize she had just wanted a fling with an older guy. You know, have some fun, get some experience, then drop me for somebody her own age."

Gordie snorted, "That's not the Gelsy I know. She's just not that kind of girl, David. I know the kind you mean, the ones who want something to play with for a while, but that's not her style." He thought very carefully. "Whenever Gelsy has decided on something she wants, she usually does get it, yes... but she always keeps it, and treasures it. Like that crucifix around your neck! It was danged expensive – a real relic from Russian nobility. But her dad knew it was something she'd fallen in love with and would always cherish. And it's the only thing I've ever known her to give away. That she gave it to you made me realize she loved you before you told me. My guess is she plans on keeping and treasuring you, too, David."

"From your mouth to God's ears, Gordie," David replied, with a bitter half-smile, thinking again of Randy.

-33-

After David had left the room the doctor walked to Gelsy's bedside and said, "I think that man loves you very much, young lady."

"Thank you, doctor. And here comes another man who loves me very much! Buba, my sweet Buba!" and she held her arms out to the pale older man being wheeled into the room.

"Well, look at my god-daughter! After giving us such a scare, she's as pink as a rose. Michael, I just might think you're not such a quack after all!" Robert was brightening up the minute he saw Gelsy smiling at him.

"Why, thank you, Robert. Nice to think all my hard work wasn't in vain. Although I have to give a lot of the credit to that new son of yours. He seems to have been the deciding factor in this girl's recovery so far."

Robert looked thoughtfully at his godchild as he parked his wheelchair by her bed and took her free hand. "Yes, Michael. I had no idea how important that young man was going to be in my life when I met him. I had a feeling he was someone special, though, and it sure seems I was right."

Gelsy looked delighted. "You picked him out just for me, Buba. How very considerate of you!"

The doctor found this highly amusing. "You two have always had a special relationship, but this takes the cake! I'll leave you to your breakfast while I make the rounds of the other patients in this hospital who seem to need me more than you do." And with a broad grin he was out the door.

Robert put both his hands on Gelsy's and said, "How very true, my dear. We always have had a very special relationship. And I'm so glad, because we can lean on each other when we both miss your mother and father in the days to come." Here his voice began to give out.

"Buba, I've been with Mama and Papa in Heaven, and I know they are very happy together there. I was happy with them, but Davey came and begged me to come back and live for him so I did, with their blessings. They don't want us to be sad, Buba. They know we'll miss them, but they don't want us to be too sad."

"And I know there's something they'd want you to know, my darling girl. Donnie and I talked about it often, what we should do if anything happened to either one of us... how we'd tell you. We even thought that now you were eighteen and a woman, especially if you were to marry and perhaps have children of your own, we had to find a way to tell you anyway..."

"Tell me what, Buba?"

"It's so hard, being the only one left, Gelsy. I never thought it could happen like this." Robert was fighting back a powerful force within him. His love for the girl and his pain over losing her parents added up to more agony than she could possibly understand, because the bonds that bound them all together went so much deeper than she knew.

"Gelsy, you know that your father and I met your mother in Paris, and that the three of us busked around Europe for several months before coming back to the United States."

"Yes, Buba. It always seemed like the three of you thought that was the happiest time of your life."

"Yes, yes it was, darling! We were young, poor, but so happy, because we were in love. Can you understand?"

"In love...?"

"With Paris, with life, with music, and most of all, with each other. We never wanted you to think it was... unnatural or strange, but your father and I both loved your mother equally. Do you understand?"

Gelsy nodded gravely. "You had a *ménage de trois*?"

"Yes, my dear. And when we brought her to America, we decided it was best that she marry Donnie, because he wanted to be married and have a stable family life, while I was more the gypsy of the group."

"But you continued to love each other?"

"Always. How could I ever stop loving a woman like your mother? And, after loving her, how could any other woman ever appeal to me? She was my only true love, except for you, of course, my dear."

"Are you saying I am really your daughter, Buba?"

"I can't say because I don't know. We made a pact not to find out until you were an adult and wanted us to find out. We were waiting for the right time to tell you, and we decided it would be before your marriage to David. If you and he wanted children, your doctors would need medical information. We would have done that for you if it had ever become necessary; luckily, it never was. Also luckily, Donnie, Adele and I all share the same blood type."

Gelsy was silent for so long Robert began to worry, but Gelsy was merely processing the information. "Buba, if you are my real father, it will make no difference. I will love you and Papa just the same. And Mama, too, of course."

"Of course, my dearest girl," Robert was overjoyed. 'You have been loved and are loved, the same as always. Except that now a new element has been added, David. From now on your love will be directed mainly at him, as it should be."

At David's name, Gelsy had turned an even healthier shade of pink. "Yes, Buba! You are right. Mama and Papa told me I should come back and live my life with him. If I'd stayed with them, he was going to end his life, you know. He has a gun, and he was going to use it if I died."

Robert's eyes opened wide and he repressed a shudder. "No, I didn't know that. I didn't know he had a gun. So I would have lost him, too? My God, how close I came to total disaster!"

"Poor Buba, I forgot, you're sick yourself! I shouldn't worry you. Everything is all right now. David is resting in his dorm room and will be back before dinner. He spent the night here with me so I could sleep, in spite of the doctor forbidding us to be in bed together."

"You didn't! Oh, Giselle Marie Grandwood, I should tell your doctor on you!" Robert was laughing now. "Don't you know Michael is very strict about hospital protocol? Don't let him catch you two doing anything more than holding hands, please!"

"He was a little huffy that Davey was in bed with me and I'd unbuttoned his shirt and was kissing his chest."

Robert roared at that, "My God in Heaven, I'm surprised he didn't call hospital security and have you *both* thrown out in the street, IVs and all!"

"But Buba, I was only trying to make sure I was still alive."

"And what conclusion did you come to, my girl?"

"That I was alive and glad of it."

"Now, that sounds so much like your mother talking, darling. There may be some doubt about your father, but never a doubt who your mother is. You have 'Adele' written all over you, my sweet."

"And I always saw in my mother's eyes that she loved you, Buba."

Later that evening when David reappeared, carrying a giant bouquet of red roses, he found her in a subdued mood. After admiring the flowers and directing a nurse to find a vase for them, she sat him down and immediately told him of the morning's discoveries. Dumbfounded, David could barely comprehend it all.

"You might be Robert's biological daughter? And he's adopting me as his son?! Doesn't this make for an impossible legal situation??"

"No I don't think so. Legally, I am Papa's daughter and always will be. We don't even need to find out for sure if Buba is my real father until we decide to have a family of our own."

"But, they were... sharing your mother?" David's mind was racing through all the evenings when he watched both men look at Adele with such adoration. "I don't think I could do that."

"They both loved her equally, and she loved them. They met her at the same time, they all became close friends. It was always like having a little family, even before I was born."

"And you never knew, really, Gelsy?"

"I guess somewhere in the back of my mind I must have suspected, but even if they had told me it wouldn't have made any difference, Davey. I understand. Love isn't always neat and easy. Sometimes it is complicated."

David looked at her and saw a woman older than eighteen. "Not many girls your age would understand such a thing, much less forgive it."

"There's nothing to forgive, Davey. They never meant to hurt me. Each one of them loved me."

"As I do, too, you know." And he had to lean over the bed to kiss her.

It was difficult, reaching over the hospital bed and worrying about all the machines she was still attached to. David only meant to give her a token kiss, just a reminder of what they'd had together, but once their lips touched he found himself longing for her again, as if they were in the back seat of her car. Slowly he slipped out of his shoes and worked his way across the bed until he was beside her again.

His lips still on hers, he pressed his body up against her, and she returned the pressure. She reached out with the free arm to pull him in as tightly as possible.

Pressing against her, he kissed her without reservation making him realize how very long it had been since they'd made love. The dress rehearsal, performance, everything that had filled the past few days had kept him in his dorm room away from her and Donald had been right, it had been hard to sleep without her now. How he longed to wake up and have her next to him.

At first he was afraid the machines she was tethered to might send out some kind of warning signal to the doctor, telling him that a man was in Gelsy's bed and possibly molesting her. But when the machines continued to hum quietly he accepted them as background noise and began to molest her in earnest. His hands went all over her body, gently searching out the cast on one leg, the stitches below the knee of the other, the bandaged ribcage. When he'd satisfied himself that her upper body, apart from the left arm with the needles attached, was still serviceable, he untied the strings on her hospital gown and slid his hands under it to caress her breasts.

He could hold her like this, with his body pressed against her bare right hip, and finally feel close to her. She had needed his body that first night in the hospital to find her way back to life, now he needed her body to find his way back to her. The time he'd spent in agony planning his own suicide had taken its toll; he needed to feel they were both going to live.

Their gentle kisses turned into the fervent kissing that usually signaled their lovemaking, and Gelsy began quietly moaning as his hand traveled from her breasts downward. Instinctively he was searching for a way to give them both pleasure despite the hospital bed and all its complications. Pushing himself up against her, his hand found that spot on her body he'd learned to love, the place he'd always think of as a beautiful little woodland creature. He began to pet it, to feel its fur. Her moaning became harsher, and he felt himself shaking, as if an electric current was passing through his body. His hand became a second sex organ as he felt her respond to it. He'd found another way to please her! Overjoyed at the feeling of power to please the woman he loved and the sensation of pressing up against her body, he realized he was on the verge of an orgasm. Quickly he found he could bring her to the same level, and together they enjoyed a release of emotion so great it brought tears to both their eyes.

Laying there together afterwards, David was only mildly afraid of being caught with her. Being close like this was worth any doctor's scolding, and he'd stay here as long as possible. Gelsy, for her part, was making the contented purring sound with her breathing that she always made after an enjoyable sexual encounter. Just listening to her made him happy. He'd come so close to losing her. Then the realization hit him with the force of a steamroller and he found himself shaking.

"My darling what is wrong?" Gelsy was hugging him as tightly as possible with her one good arm but pulling back slightly to look at his face.

"Don't look at me," was all he could say, as he rolled away from her on the bed and buried his head in his arms. Memories of holding Randy and begging him to put himself back together again came flooding back. He couldn't cry then. Suddenly the gates opened and the years of holding tears back were gone. Holding her and knowing she'd stay with him had evened the score. Finally he could grieve.

As she rubbed his back with her free arm, he haltingly told her the story of his dead friend.

How, no matter what David said, Randy couldn't put himself back together. She grieved with him. Never having known Randy, she realized how much the young soldier had meant to her beloved Davey and she grieved over his death with as much pain as he felt himself. Seeing her cry over Randy's death reminded him that she had just lost her parents, and he turned to her so they could grieve together.

After the passion and the release of grief they stayed laying close together, completely exhausted but feeling closer than they'd ever felt. There was a new level to their love. It didn't include just the two of them anymore, but everything that had gone before. They were sharing each other's lives and forming a bond of trust like David had never known existed. He felt he could tell her anything.

But they could hear the food cart rattling down the hall and knew the nurse would be bringing her dinner in soon. Reluctantly David moved away from her.

"Oh, no. Not yet!" She tried to hold him with one arm, but he gently slid away from her.

"Only so you can eat, girl. You've lost too much weight already, and I'm going to make sure you eat everything on your tray so you'll get well really fast and get out of here." David smiled at her and kissed her free hand just as the nurse came through the door.

"Well, look at the two lovebirds," she said merrily. "And I'm betting you've been good about the doctor's orders?" She raised an eyebrow over the rumpled sheets.

"Oh yes, ma'am." Gelsy was so innocent but gleeful. "Haven't we, Davey?"

"Young lady, I just want to see you eat your dinner so I don't have to feed it to you," her blushing boyfriend replied, putting on his shoes as the nurse beat a hasty but giggling retreat.

"Oh, yuck!" Gelsy flinched at the drab plate of steamed meat and vegetables under the metal cover David had just lifted. "Am I supposed to eat *that*?"

"Every bite. Would you like me to feed it to you?"

"No thanks. At least I have my right arm free. When are they going to take all these needles out anyway?" and she continued complaining through every bite of dinner.

Just as she was finishing, the doctor came through the door. "Aha! My boy, you've gotten her to eat a hospital dinner, you *are* amazing! We must talk about that change of major to medicine one of these days. Now why don't you pop next door and tell Robert I'll be over to see him next?"

With an obliging grin David squeezed Gelsy's shoulder and took off like a shot. "And you, my lovely," here the doctor softened and turned to Gelsy, who had just finished her last spoonful of chocolate pudding, "How are you feeling this evening?"

"I am feeling quite well and very anxious to be disconnected from all these machines. Please, please sir, tell me the needles can come out."

"As a matter of fact, I was going to suggest that very thing. A girl who can wolf down an entire dinner doesn't need to be connected to a heart monitor or a saline drip. OK, hold on, out they come…" And in less than a minute she was free.

The doctor rang for the nurses to remove the machines just as David returned, a look of relief passing over his face as he saw the IVs and oxygen tank were being hauled away. "Young lady," the doctor continued, "if you continue to improve at this rate, I'll have to kick you out of the hospital pretty soon to make room for really sick people. I definitely will kick you out of ICU, probably tomorrow."

"Oh, what good news! And in my new room can I request a double bed?" Gelsy asked coyly.

"My dear girl," and here he eyed David, "the next time I catch you in bed with a man, he'd better be wearing one of these," and here he indicated his own wedding ring.

"I'm trying sir," David joked back, "Check her out today and I'll have her at the altar tomorrow!"

Later that evening, before Gordie came in Robert's car to take David back to the dorm, Gelsy said, "Would you really marry me tomorrow, Davey?"

"Girl, you know I would," was all he could say, hanging over her like the love-stricken man he really was.

"Then let's marry here, in the hospital, in the chapel, before I check out. That way we can go home together as man and wife."

"Gelsy, what kind of wedding is that for you? I thought you wanted a big church affair!"

"Not without Mama and Papa. I know they are together, Davey, and they love us both and want us to be happy. But I couldn't face a big wedding without having them there. I would prefer a small, quiet affair with just us, Buba, Gordie and Mark. Would that be alright with you?"

"You know anywhere, anytime is alright with me, girl," and he kissed her to seal the bargain.

And so, two weeks later, just released from the hospital and leaning heavily on both Mark and Gordie's arms while Robert played the "Wedding Song" on his guitar, Gelsy was seen waltzing barefoot down the aisle of the chapel to meet a very grateful David at the altar.

And she was wearing her Juliet costume for a wedding gown.